YOU ARE HERE
THIS IS NOW

The Best Young Writers
and Artists in America

A *PUSH* ANTHOLOGY

GO THERE.

OTHER TITLES AVAILABLE FROM PUSH

Cut
PATRICIA McCORMICK

I Will Survive
KRISTEN KEMP

Kerosene
CHRIS WOODING

Pure Sunshine
BRIAN JAMES

You Remind Me of You
EIREANN CORRIGAN

YOU ARE HERE THIS IS NOW

The Best Young Writers and Artists in America

A ANTHOLOGY

edited by David Levithan

SCHOLASTIC INC.

NEW YORK   TORONTO   LONDON   AUCKLAND   SYDNEY
MEXICO CITY   NEW DELHI   HONG KONG   BUENOS AIRES

ISBN 0-439-37618-1

All rights reserved. Published by PUSH, an imprint of Scholastic Inc., 557 Broadway, New York, NY 10012.

SCHOLASTIC and associated logos are trademarks and/or registered trademarks of Scholastic Inc.

12 11 10 9 8 7 6 5 4 3 2   3 4 5 6 7/0

Printed in the U.S.A.   40
First Scholastic/PUSH printing, April 2002

Editor's Note

"Accidents and inspiration lead you to your destination"
                              —Mary Chapin Carpenter, *The Long Way Home*

This is a book of accidents and inspirations. The sudden fall or slow burn of love. The mystery of being born into a family where you can't quite find your place, and the flashpoint of revelation when the past becomes momentarily clear. The absurdity of words, characters, and the college admissions process. The startling exhilaration of an image caught in a mirror, a lens, a sideways glance.

Destination is an ongoing thing. For a writer or an artist, there is no final place. There are only stops along the way. You are here, but you won't always be. This is now, but that soon will have passed.

We are catching these artists and writers at early destinations, at the time when the here and the now begin to lose their immortality, and the scope of the journey begins to take hold.

The stories, poems, essays, and art in this anthology were all chosen from the hundreds of winners of the 1999, 2000, and 2001 Scholastic Art & Writing Awards. All of the writers and artists are middle school or high school students. Their remarkable talent is for showing their here and now from a variety of angles.

Special thanks to the people who helped this book reach its own destination: Nicole Cohen, B. J. Adler, Chuck Wentzel, and all the other wonderful people at the Scholastic Art & Writing Awards; the PUSH team, including our amazing art director, Steve Scott, and our divine production editor, Bonnie Cutler; and Joy Peskin, Matt Ringler, Susan Ashley, and the other people who helped me review the thousands of pages of past award-winners.

Our highest gratitude goes to the writers and artists whose work is collected here. Thank you for sharing your accidents and inspirations. I, for one, cannot wait to see what your next destinations will be.

—David Levithan

For more information about PUSH, please go to
www.thisispush.com

To find out more about the
Scholastic Art & Writing Awards, check out
www.scholastic.com

Table of Contents

Remorse for Being Young,
Written in a Kroger Parking Lot

Being angry at the world has its ups and downs.
I realize this as I'm leaving Kroger and
there's a guy in a torn leather jacket
crushing a Toyota with a sledgehammer.

Everyone in the parking lot has stopped to look at him.
His face is as red as the car he's beating.
Pieces of glass are flying everywhere.

And I'm fifteen again.
The backyard is an empty battlefield
underneath a good October sky.
Marching ghosts in crimson uniforms
disappear in and out of smoke
as I nurse wounds
with a cigarette under a large oak tree.
The sun is bouncing off the chain-linked fence.
The air is stale and brown like a seventies movie.

I'm thinking of passing trees on the highway.
I'm thinking of thumbing rides all the way to New York,
sleeping like icicles underneath an overpass.
Melting by candlelight in a girl's arms.
But here the hard skin of oak trees will rub your back raw

and white cigarette smoke clouds and burns your eyes.
Here I'll never know what changes when you leave.

I clutch a dirty fist and run. I'm fifteen.
I'm an empty battlefield.
I'll go where the marching ghosts will take me.
When I die I'll be with the trees.

— Scott Miles

I am searching for creativity personified that I can exercise vaguely AND I am searching for the voices in my head AND I am searching for the one that's hiding somewhere behind my tonsils that peeks out occasionally to remind me it's still hiding. I am searching unsuccessfully for the difference between me and everyone else AND I am searching for something more optimistic than complacency AND I am searching for something just beyond my reach and comprehension. I am searching for satisfaction AND I am searching for the place where denial and complications intersect with a better outlook than my own AND I am searching for unobtrusive sympathy. I am searching for appreciation in a mythic society that rewards being nice AND I am searching for a very specific point of subject matter in intergalactic space AND I am searching for the next exit from loneliness. I am searching for unadulterated success AND I am searching for a mechanism to keep me aware. I am searching to be aware AND I am still searching for myself.

— Ian Ferguson

Ice Cream Sundae

The buzzer is ringing out front.

It's always ringing. Every time I sit down and get comfortable, when I finally think I'm going to make it past tired, dog-eared page 286, the buzzer rings and I'm up and I'm running and I'm ready to go serve ice cream to whatever lost soul has walked up to my window. This time I really have to though because Tess just ran out to pick up sandwiches for dinner because Tess always picks up sandwiches for dinner because Tess is obsessed with food.

So I grab an apron and tie the flimsy blue strings around my ever-expanding stomach and yank at the loop around my neck because it feels like a noose. I walk to the front and hope that it's not a whole mob of rich people just getting back from some huge dinner party at some fancy restaurant, which will just remind me of how poor and pathetic I am. Although sometimes the young preppy guys tip well because they're trying to impress their young preppy dates like they have to prove they have money to just throw around or something. Or maybe they just feel bad for me because they know, other than the extra nickels and dimes they throw into my coffee cup by the window, I get shit pay and no benefits and am scooping their ice cream for the sheer reason I have no other choice.

But it doesn't even matter because it's a family of four outside at the window with their golden retriever on a leash next to them and their shining Jeep Cherokee parked in the lot. They have two little girls who look so close in age I wonder if the mother even got a chance to recover after she popped the first one out. They're both blond-haired and blue-eyed with rosy little cheeks and pudgy little baby legs. They look like they don't give their parents a moment's trouble and they play nicely and their grandmother buys them a new Barbie doll each Christmas. Their mommy is real pretty, too. She has dark, dark hair, which I'm sure she dyes to keep from going gray like my mom always does. The father has glasses and his socks are pulled up a little too high, leaving a whole three inches of visible skin below his too tight khaki shorts, so I figure the only way he could look like that much of a nerd is if he's a doctor, which probably explains the Ralph Lauren polo shirts and the SUV.

The woman turns to her husband and whispers something in his ear. They wave to me, then pick up one of the kids, and the entire gang moves inside.

The door is triggered to ring when someone comes in and it's much shriller than the buzzer at the window. If I had nightmares — if I had dreams at all — that door buzzer would be the main focus. I hate that they came inside. I like it better when people order from the window. That way they can't see my stomach and they don't treat me like I'm stupid or something.

They're staring at the sign like their lives depend on which flavor of ice cream they order and it's so nail-biting for me I want to tell them that if it comes down to it I can put more than one kind on each cone. One of the little girls is hanging on the counter, so I can just barely see the tips of her fingers as the rest of her is hidden underneath.

The man asks if it's okay that they brought the dog in and I tell him it's fine and ask him how he's doing today and he says he's okay but he wishes that it would rain because his lawn is looking like a Triscuit. I nod but know that this weather has been better for business and that people usually don't want ice cream if it's raining.

The mother is staring at the dripping cabinet in front of me. We have some good flavors today: mocha chunk, peanut butter cup, cherry vanilla. And pistachio. That's my favorite. I know a lot of people don't like it, but lately I have a constant craving for it. She points out the cherry vanilla to one of the little girls.

"Look at that one, Lizzie." I follow her pointed finger and see a glob of chocolate among the black cherry chunks. When they're gone I should clean up the freezer a little.

The little girl pulls herself up to the edge, pressing her palms to the glass. From my side of the cabinet I can see the underside of hands, the smooth ridges and hills. Her fingers are tiny, smaller than I can ever imagine my own being. The skin turns white, she's pressing so hard against the glass.

The mother pulls her away. "You're going to leave handprints, honey."

The father has been reading the signs above my head. "Where do you keep your water ice?"

I turn around to the counter behind me, pulling up two little handles on either side. "We have a freezer right here. Water ices have to be kept at a colder temperature than regular ice cream because of the fact they're made with a water base rather than milk."

They look taken aback. Most people see teenage blond and assume dumb. Most people see pregnant and assume whore.

One of the kids is pointing to the chocolate, murmuring and whining and trying to get her parents' attention. Mom and Dad finally turn to look at her and toss her appeasing words. "All right, if that's what you want."

The man looks at me and says, "Can we have one small chocolate cone?"

I smile back, but I know it's not real because as nice as these people seem and as cute as their kids are, they aren't doing anything to help me. I take a napkin and wrap it around a cone, gripping the smallest scoop and lunging for the freezer. It's harder to reach to the back now that I'm beginning to show. The belly gets in the way and I've found the best thing to do is just attack the thing head-on and grab for whatever flavor I want and try to work as fast as I can.

I hear a muffled question from above. "What's the difference between gelato and water ice?"

I put a scoop on the cone and try to press it down as hard as I can so it won't fall off and I won't have to give her another free cone like they tell us to when that happens to little kids. I struggle out of the freezer and as I'm cleaning the scooper I give the same answer to the same question I get on average 3.3 times a day.

"Water ice, in essence, is made of water and special flavorings. Gelato is a traditional Italian dessert, made with seventy-five percent water and twenty-five percent whole milk. In general, it's much richer than water ice and often has a juicy, fruit flavoring."

"Oh." People usually don't have a response for that. I hand

the cone to the mother, who then hands it to the little girl, who then nearly drops it on the floor, which I just mopped this morning.

While the mother tries to prevent disaster, the father orders for himself. "Okay, I think I'll have a medium mocha chunk — but can I have that in a dish?"

I tell him sure and reach for the medium scoop and a bowl. I stare into the dipping cabinet, looking at the mocha chunk, which is fortunately close enough that I don't have to kill myself to get it. And as I do I steam over his incessant questions about water ice and gelato and things that it seems that anybody who spent eight years in college should know. Sometimes I wonder if people ask those questions to see if I'll trip up, if I'll flounder and roll like the beached whale I'm becoming.

I hand him the dish and hope he drops it all over his car's brand-new leather interior. "Will there be anything else?"

The mother is conferring with her other little angel. A solar eclipse later she looks up. "Can we get a strawberry milkshake?"

I nod. I wish I could tell her no but I know I can't so I don't and I stand on my tiptoes to reach the shelf where we keep the steel milkshake containers. You know, the ones that hang on that machine that's kinda like a blender but not, because it makes more of a mess and is impossible to clean up. I put the strawberry flavoring in and then the ice cream even though you're suppose to put the milk in first because there's this line at the bottom of the cup that shows how much you pour in and you can't see it when the ice cream is there. But at this point I really don't care and most people can't tell a quality milkshake from a crummy one. My back is to them. I'm not sure what to do next and I'm not sure how to do it and I'm not sure what's going to happen when I do.

I just take the plunge and walk from behind the dipping cabinet over to the refrigerator on the other side of the room. I feel naked and exposed and I'm sure all of them are staring at me. I grab the milk, dashing back to my hiding space like some stupid, scared rabbit trying to cross the interstate in the middle of rush hour.

But in the end it doesn't help because the same little girl who I thought was cute two seconds ago points at me and says, "Baby."

I've turned around again so I can't see the parents' faces but I know what they're thinking and I know the looks they're giving each other. I see them every day. Every time I walk down the street or through the mall or when I serve someone their innocent strawberry milkshake. I pour the milk. If my life were a soap opera I'd spill it all over because my hands are trembling so much. Except it's not and I don't and they aren't. I hook the container to the machine and I hear the hum and swish and rattle of a milkshake in the process of being made. I pray I've put enough milk in or enough ice cream or enough anxiety to make a decent shake. I face the family again, leaning against the counter, so my stomach sticks out even more. "Is that going to be everything?"

I don't look the mother in the eye. There's a poster above her head with this demented ten-year-old boy eating a vanilla cone and holding his little puppy on a leash. On the top it says in big red letters, "Eat More." I don't think I've ever seen it before. When Tess comes back with dinner I'll ask her about it. Of course, by that time I'll probably forget it's even there and I won't notice it again until I'm faced with another wonderfully awkward situation.

Then out of nowhere the lady with the dark, dark hair and the little blond girls and the nerdy husband asks, "So when are you due?"

And the way she says it makes it sound like a different question from the one I get almost as often as the gelato–water-ice debate. Her voice hums and sings as she says it like this baby is a good thing. Like I should be happy about it. Like it shouldn't matter that I had to drop out of school and that I'm only seventeen and that Daddy hates me now and Mommy thinks I was asking for this to happen. Like it's going to be fun being a mother or something.

And it feels like when you sit out in the sun and you close your eyes and you can feel the heat on your body, in your blood, and the rays are behind your eyes and it lights up your lids so it's bright like heaven's supposed to be. It's light like whip cream but sweet like chocolate sauce.

Usually when people mention it I want to tell them a whole list of things in my own defense. Like that I used to be an honor student and I was supposed to be an environmental lawyer. And that I only had sex a few times before and then the condom broke one night so it's not like I was being irresponsible. And that I would have had an abortion, I got so scared I told Mom and of course she wouldn't let me. And that I hate scooping ice cream and I would do anything not to do it for the rest of my life.

But with this lady I don't have to and I don't want to because I just look her in the eye and she knows it all.

"Middle of October."

I realize I forgot about the milkshake so I whip around and I grab the steel container. It's slippery with dew dripping all down the sides. I reach for a large soda cup and pour the shake in. It's perfectly blended, no lumps and with little red strawberry specks. Perfection. I put a lid on the top and hand it to them. "That's going to be all?"

The lady points to one of the girls. "Yeah, she'll never finish this. I'll just drink the rest." She grins at me with a knowing look like I'll be doing the same thing soon.

I ring things up on the defective, damned cash register and give them the price and the man hands me a ten. I make change, but by the time I look around the lady is out the door, her dog and one of her daughters in tow. It's the one I gave the cone to. By this time she has chocolate all over her face and on her hands and I think she has some in her hair. She waves to me as she closes the shop door. The man is waiting for me to give him the change so I do and say, "Have a nice day."

He looks at me with caring eyes and replies, "You, too, and good luck." For some reason when he cocks his head toward my belly I don't get mad and instead I feel like crying with the sheer niceness of it all.

I begin to wipe up the mess I made with the milkshake and I hear the ring of the door buzzer followed by the sharp clang of coins hitting the bottom of a coffee cup. The tip jar outside. I glance up to see him walking away from the window and opening the passenger door to his Cherokee. They drive away and I finish with the excess ice cream spillage.

I take the container I made the shake in to the back and add it to the pile of dishes. Patting my tummy, I pick up my book, read over page 286, and wait for Tess to come back with dinner.

— Sarah Major

Practice

At home I practice being a skank,
drawing curves above my eyelashes
with a thin stick of brown.

I choose from sixteen shades of red,
slowly coloring the lips
with a brush appropriately too tiny for the job.

I pose in my underwear,
pretending it's a striped bikini
or strip and wrap a towel into a strapless dress,
gathering the dense loops of thread
at my waist behind me,
keeping elbows pressed into ribs
to hold the garment up.

The towel has CENDANT printed across
in crayon yellow —
a free gift from my father's cubicle village.

I can see his moustached manager
distributing beach towels under fluorescent lights
to the all-male computer department
after being ordered to promote company spirit.
Each man must have found the towel
too large to be stuffed into a bag;

maybe some abandoned it.
But my father carried it home
folded in a square,
a little embarrassed by its swirling cyan border
against his dark pants, and left it on the couch
for his daughter
to practice being a skank.

— Rona Jia Luo

"An Old-fashioned Pressing"

I see Miss Ella once every two weeks. More often if it's been humid. The Afro was trying to make a comeback but it hasn't. Since I don't have a perm Miss Ella and her hot comb straighten out my hair every other Saturday. A good old-fashioned pressing, she calls it.

I don't know how old she is, younger than my grandma but older than my mother. I asked her once while reading a Chinese restaurant place mat that tells what animal sign you were born under. Patting myself on the back for being so sly about it, I said, "Oh, 1981 is the year of the cock, so I'm vain and passionate. What animal are you?"

"A dove," she said.

"Miss Ella, that's not on here."

"So?"

She's confusing like that. If I had to guess, I'd say she's fifty-nine. Miss Ella talks about herself in puzzle pieces. If you are around her enough she'll give you a piece here, two pieces there. They're never in order so it's up to you to put them together. Sometimes she throws in pieces from other puzzles just to shake things up. Once she said, "Ole Miss Ella was supposed to give Rosa Parks a ride home the day she wouldn't get up for that white man. But there was a shoe sale at JCPenney's and I left work early. Rosa had to take the bus. She was probably so mad at me she forgot about being scared of that bus driver. Lucky thing the boycott was successful because Rosa had a temper and I would have been in trouble."

Years of seeing her every other weekend have taught me this

much about her. I know she grew up down south during Jim Crow when the water fountains were segregated because she's always telling me that the black water tasted better anyway. She was married once to a man she calls "Sugar" but his real name is James. He has been gone for a while though because she's lived alone for as long as I can remember. I know she's been to Tijuana because I've seen the bus ticket. She doesn't have any plane tickets. Her reasoning is that if you have to get somewhere *that* fast, then something bad must be waiting for you. You're better off staying home. I told her that was ridiculous because I was going to have to take planes to California since that's where I want to go to college.

"I wouldn't go down there," she said. "Too many lizards."

"There aren't lizards in California. You're thinking about Florida."

"Lizards are everywhere."

"Not here."

"More here than in California."

"What?"

"Must be, or you wouldn't want to leave."

Miss Ella is an enigma. People always want to say she's senile because that's easier than trying to figure her out. Asking her to explain herself is a waste of time because she won't. I think she figures that anyone who is not bright enough to understand her words doesn't deserve her wisdom.

I could tell Miss Ella was upset the other day because she kept snatching my head and didn't even tell me to hold my ear down when the hot comb was near it. "Girl, you better believe that stuff about free milk and unsold cows," she said, shaking

16

her head. "That was a sweet, sweet girl. She would've been a great newswoman, like the lady on Channel 10. What's that woman's name? Janice? Jane? Last name sounds like some kind of a bug."

"Janet Lomax?"

"But who's gonna watch the baby? The news is on late at night. His daddy sure ain't gonna be around. Who's gonna keep the baby?"

I said that Channel 10 might have a program for single working mothers, but she didn't hear me. "A little sip of milk never hurt anyone," she said, "but you girls have got to learn the difference between a spoonful and a jug." I looked over at the men's boots that I think belong to the UPS man who brings her Chinese food occasionally. She must have seen my eyebrows rise because she laughed and said, "Coffee cups, child, coffee cups. And besides, this cow ain't for sale."

A lot of her advice concerns men. That's nice, especially when I can convince her to be concerned with my sixteen-year-old relationship problems.

"Oh, Miss Ella, Darnell was supposed to call me last night and he didn't."

"Stop moving your head."

"But Miss Ella, I don't know what to do, he's so nice sometimes and other times . . ."

"Did you want curls all over your head or just in the back?"

"Just in the back. . . . And last time we went out he called some girl on his cellular phone."

"Those things give you brain cancer."

"I wish he would get brain cancer."

17

"Did you tell him that?"

"No, I acted like I didn't care. We're not going out and he can talk to other girls, but right in front of me? That's not right."

"You and me have got the same spirit. Too proud to let people know they get under our skin. Do you know, Sugar never brought me flowers on my birthday? And I was with that man longer than you are old. I never told him. I just put too much pepper in his food."

"Lindsey says I'm letting him walk all over me and I'm supposed to be a feminist. I shouldn't like him, but he eats his fries with a fork and he calls me 'sweetie' and I do."

"Why'd he call the girl?"

"I don't know, to find out about some party or something."

"I didn't ask why he talked to her, I asked why he called her. He could have done it when you weren't there. He wanted you to see him do it. Now why did he call her?"

"To make me jealous?"

"So be happy he thinks you're worth making jealous, and think about your homework."

If I ever let her read this I can just imagine the conversation we'll have.

"Who says I'm senile?"

"Um, nobody. It was an — English assignment! And senile was a required vocabulary word."

"Hmmmm. And why'd you change my name?"

"I thought you would want me to protect your privacy."

"Good. We can't have Mr. Owens finding out about my UPS man. Where'd you get Miss Ella?"

"It was my great-grandma's name."

"That's fine, she was a good woman."

"You never met her."

"So? And Honey, that's true about me and Rosa Parks. I've still got the shoes."

— Erica Bryant

As Beautiful As

That was the year I had five candles on my cake, and "Hanna" was scrawled out in purple icing. Candle flames bounced against the air, and light trailed toward the ceiling in thin lines. I felt an emptiness after I blew out those candles, and I clapped my hands at the smoky shadows as if trying to capture what was already gone.

We went to see the sun set that night. My dad let me sit on his knee while the sun streaked and split across the sky. The orange was like the fire on my cake, and it blazed behind trees like a splintering feather. All the blue and purple colors fuzzed out on the long, dark thing my dad called the horizon. "Take a picture," I begged, and my mouth felt small compared to the whole sky and all its air.

When the photograph came back, the colors were all wrong. The sky edges looked hazy instead of sharp with reds and yellows. The photographed clouds lost their textures, and the sun itself looked weak and unimportant. I thought the camera must be broken, but Dad said, "That's just the way it came out. It's not as beautiful as a real sunset, but it's the closest we can get." Holding the picture in my hand, I saw a fake sun and fake light cutting into my fingers.

That was also the year I watched pill bugs bury in the dirt under our porch. Their round bodies pushed smoothly into the soft brown. Seth came over sometimes. He had a gap between his front teeth and threw dirt at me when he was bored. "Now you're all messy!" he would yell, triumphant. I wondered how this thing called dirt could be so bad when pill bugs plowed through it with their sad gray backs. I tried drawing the dirt and pill bugs in school when the teacher gave us crayons. I ended up with brown scribbles on my page, and Seth laughed at me with the air between his teeth.

Back then stars were like angels to me. I stared at clear night skies until the blackness swam at my eyes and spun out spirals of stars. A night sky was a huge thing like the horizon that stretched out and circled me with air. I saw shooting stars fall like the dying candles on my birthday cake, wisps of something beautiful torn away.

At fourteen, I learned to stop painting sunsets because I could never get the colors right. I stuck with still-life subjects: a bowl of fruit, an old rocking chair, the smoke detector in the upstairs hallway. I painted the things that didn't matter in case I took away their beauty.

My art teacher challenged me to paint portraits, to paint people. On one Sunday afternoon I weakened and asked my mother to pose for me. She sat stiffly but smiled, and strands of hair fell into her eyes. I had all the brushes in front of me, but I couldn't bring myself to paint her. Later, in the bathroom, I rubbed at my eyelids and stared into the mirror. Not as beautiful as the original.

Seth still lived nearby, but he had braces that were slowly closing his tooth gap. He looked at all my paintings of fruit and furniture and asked me to paint him. "Paint me, Hanna," he'd say. "I want to see how you see me." I refused without reason, not telling him that my paints would ruin the cinnamon coloring of his eyes, the texture of his hair.

They say fourteen is a difficult age for boys. Seth stopped asking me to paint him. Seth stopped coming by my house. Sometimes we passed each other in school and he would look at me, and maybe there was a small greeting in his face, but we always kept walking.

They say fourteen is an even more difficult age for girls. Boys noticed my changing body as I tried to ignore it. The ungraceful movements of new hips kept me stumbling. I didn't understand how trees could be skinny straight up with indifference.

I discovered that boys with cars made me feel older. They took me on drives through wild countryside, and I let their cars pull me farther away from my canvas and paint. I learned not to discuss art. "Oh, you paint?" a boy said once, and before I could nod he leaned across the car seat and kissed me.

One boy was more romantic and asked if I liked stargazing. "I like looking at stars," I said, and with that single, silly sentence I felt the tilt of a horizon and the slide of a thousand stars. In some dark memory I recalled the sensation of stars raining down on me from the sky in a rush of light and shadow. But by then stars felt like just stars, and I saw no flood of shimmering silver against blackness.

I tried to paint the night sky but it turned out horribly wrong, and I remembered why I stopped painting sunsets. No matter how well I painted something, I felt I was stealing some of its real beauty to call my own. I painted an oak tree bending to the wind, but it was nothing compared to the real trunk and the real leaves. When I realized that I would never be able to paint the sound of wind ripping through branches, I put my paints away.

Seth and I outgrew our awkward stages and realized we could talk about everything. On the night after my eighteenth birthday we sat in an elementary school playground. We kicked at the mulch under the swings and reminisced about earlier times.

"I don't think you changed much since we were five years old," I said.

He took it without laughter. "I know that you've changed," he said. "You were such a weird kid. I remember you used to always play with dirt."

I laughed, but I felt the slow-creeping memory of sitting in coolness under the porch. Gray pill bugs with their somber and invisible eyes, forever plowing through dirt soft as breath.

"And you were always so into art," Seth went on. "When was the last time you painted, anyway?"

"Hasn't been in years." I was trying to shake the memory of that smooth dirt and its gentle dwellers. "Who cares about painting, anyway?"

"You do," Seth said. "But what I'm saying is that I still want you to paint my portrait someday."

That night I realized my confusion about love, because I wasn't sure if I fell in love with Seth or with the vague memories of who I once was and what I once felt. All I know is that on that night, I watched Seth spin himself in circles like a little boy. He stretched out his arms and let his feet twist up the playground grass as he turned against the night air. He bent his neck back, probably to view the spread of stars in that sky. And when he was dizzy enough, he fell backward as though nothing could injure him, or maybe he believed that school-ground grass could catch as well as any net. When he was on his back and breathing at the sky, I wondered if the stars were spiraling down to meet him. I wondered if he heard the sound of trees caught in wind. And I asked myself why couldn't I do the same; why could I no longer free myself to the horizon, at least for the stars?

What I told Seth was true; I hadn't painted in years. But I still knew the exact location of my hidden art supplies. Every few months I lifted out some tubes of paint, still sealed and new, and I would remember. Seeing the packets of color reminded me what I needed to keep constrained. And when I saw sunsets, shooting stars, or willow trees, I only sensed an emptiness, only saw scenes I could not paint.

Days after the night in the park, I could still see Seth spinning behind the shadows of my closed eyes. It made me angry at his arms, jealous of his feet. He kept coming to my house, and I let him despite the distance between us, despite the fact that he could wind himself under the sky and I couldn't.

He came over the day the weather changed, when breath became visible in soft, smoky puffs. We stood outside on my lawn, and our feet crushed the frozen grass.

"I think you should paint me," he said. He was always saying it. "Paint me, Hanna." And then: "What are you afraid of?"

"I'm not afraid of anything," I said. "I'm just not an artist anymore. I don't have the need to create anything." Lies came out so easily. I thought of how Seth went spinning beneath the stars, and in my jealousy I decided he deserved the lies.

When it happened, I didn't know why he did it. Seth pulled a camera from his coat, grabbed me, and aimed it at our faces. The click sent me into a panic. "What are you doing?" I pushed myself away from him and blinked into the weak, amber sunlight.

He smiled. "I'll show it to you when it's developed," he said. Vaguely, I remembered another picture that was developed all wrong. I looked at Seth's eyes, at the turquoise sky, at the sunlight, and I imagined all that color ruined by a click and a flash.

"I hope you're using good film," I said, and I felt ridiculous. "I mean, the colors could get really messed up if you're not careful."

He looked at me seriously. "Black and white."

Black and white. Stars, moon, sky.

Leaves dropped from trees so I stopped worrying about the wind and its sounds. I was glad when clouds came to cover the sky. The clouds reached down right to the horizon and stuck all the way around. The horizon was especially thick a few days later when Seth called me. "I have the picture," he said. "Let's go back to the elementary school."

By then the playground mulch was hard with frost and coldness. For some reason I wanted to smack my hands around a jungle-gym bar and freeze myself to the playground forever. But Seth said, "Here," and put the photograph in my hand. He left me and walked toward the swing set; the back of his shoulders dipped up and down as he went.

The photograph was black and white with all sorts of grays. Seth's face was crooked from the camera angle, and his right temple wasn't even in the picture. He smiled but not too much, and the top of his hair stuck up a little.

In that picture, I was looking somewhere far away from the camera. My mouth was slack and looked heavy, dark. Some of my hair was plastered against my ear, and my cheeks looked pale and hollow.

I hated that photograph. All the blacks and grays looked too right. My face was full of angry white sparks, and it was beautiful. I thought of flying sparks, real ones with color, and at that moment it started to snow. The first thin flakes soared in front of me, and then a single snowflake landed on the picture, right in Seth's black pupil. I could see the feathery edges of the snowflake, and it ripped me back to a sunset from thirteen years ago, when red sunlight exploded against purple skies and orange clouds. In my memory, the sky cracked from those colors, and they flooded across the horizon in broad streaks.

As I remembered the haze of a sunset from a dozen years ago, I decided it didn't have to be something that dies away. Shooting stars don't have to fall, they can fly.

It began snowing harder, and I saw Seth swinging through it all, laughing. And I realized what it all meant, that stars and snowflakes are the same and they are flying to the same place. I had snowflakes soaking into my hair, and they froze me out of whatever coma I was in. I knew, suddenly, that the horizon was still some long, dark thing stretching over the world, and that I couldn't let it slip away from me again.

"Seth," I called, and I had to lean against the falling snow to push my way over to him. "I can paint you now." Wind whipped at me until my hands flung away from my sides, and I felt ready to soar someplace wonderful. I got hit with enough air and snow to be able to see the painting I needed to create. I would paint the stars in Seth's eyes exactly how he saw them that one night, and he would be as beautiful as he was when he lay breathing on the grass. And if I thought I had loved him then, it didn't matter. Between Seth's night with the sky and my life with the sky, I was sure I could paint something that would make the sunsets sing.

"I said I'll paint you," and my voice was shaky with the newness of the words.

Seth kept swinging, laughing at the snow or stars or whatever it was that poured over us.

— Laura Walter

Encierillo

The officials at Pamplona
told me that a girl couldn't run in the streets
with all the men —
I'd get trampled in the front
or left behind in the back.
I explained about my cross-country championship
and the six years I ran track,
but I would only be allowed
to watch from the sides,
not even the inner fence
where the first aid stations were.

Once I arrived in America,
I felt I was cheating every time I passed
a man on the interstate.
It was the seventh day
of the seventh month
of my eighteenth year
when I pulled over into the emergency lane,
stepped out into the dirt,
and ran with my own bulls.

— Kristen Shaw

Vee-o'la

Q: What is the range of a viola?

A: About thirty feet, if you kick it hard enough.

Viola, from Italian *violar*. A stringed instrument of the violin family, slightly larger than a violin, tuned a fifth lower, and having a deeper tone. Pronounced *vee-o'la*, not to be confused with the flower, *vi-o'la*, or with the French *voilà*. Nothing annoys violists more than hearing the name of our beloved instrument mispronounced, except possibly being told those stupid viola jokes.

Q: How do you know there's a viola section at your door?

A: No one knows when to come in.

We violists are the ones restlessly sitting to the side of the orchestra next to the cellos, with our simple, boring harmony parts any half-witted violinist could play. The first violins and the cellos have their solos, the seconds can play along with the firsts, and the basses, who have parts even worse than ours, are almost always insane. So the viola section is alone in the orchestra, suffering with our half notes and eighteen-measure rests, and having only our stand partners for comfort as the conductor orders us to play louder. It's marked *pianissimo*, but those stupid violins are playing too loudly. My stand partner agrees. We are always right; everyone else is wrong.

Q: Define a true gentleman.

A: One who can play the viola, and won't.

I have been a violist for my entire musical career, ever since we first signed up for our instruments in fourth grade. I have always read the alto clef, I have always suffered in the maddeningly repetitive but always popular Pachelbel's Canon with the eight-note viola part, I have always been hollered at to play louder. I lug around my fifteen-pound viola case with pride. Yes, I am a violist, and I love it.

Q: What is the difference between a viola and a vacuum cleaner?

A: A vacuum cleaner has to be plugged in before it sucks.

The history of music has been plagued with blatant viola discrimination. During the Baroque era, when the bows were curved the other way and chin rests were a new fad, musicians who couldn't play the violin part switched to the viola. Handel, Bach, and the rest of the Baroque gang made the viola a third violin or a second-cello part, not even considering to write solo viola pieces. Who would want to listen to a third-rate musician trying to screech out a viola concerto?

The personnel manager broke up an altercation during intermission between the principal oboist and the principal violist. When asked what the problem was, the oboist said that the violist had knocked his reeds all over the floor. "He had it coming," blustered the violist. "He tuned down one of my pegs, and now he won't tell me which one!"

Because of the rise of great viola soloists such as Lionel Tertis, William Primrose, Yuri Bashmet, and other viola celebrities, we have accumulated a repertoire of modern compositions (most written by friends of violists who were tired of listening to us complain about not having enough good music) and many arrangements of pieces written for other instruments during those less enlightened times. Bach's cello suites are now an octave higher for us; Brahms's clarinet sonatas have been transcribed. However, the prejudice remains.

Q: You are lost in the desert. You come upon a good violist, a bad violist, and a large white rabbit. Which of the three do you ask for directions?

A: The bad violist. The other two are mirages.

Most violists I know are violin converts, those who became sick of being only the associate concertmaster, or an All-State alternate. Trying the viola for the first time, the violinists are always surprised, saying it's so loud, so deep, so pretty. I have known all along. We violists prefer to keep it a well-guarded secret, keeping our numbers down so we can all get good seats in orchestra and get into the elite music schools, which are always in dire need of us. The violinist, the cellist, the trumpeter, and the flutist may laugh now, but they are a dime a dozen. We violists are exquisitely rare.

Q: What is the difference between a snake and a viola in the road?

A: There are skid marks in front of the snake.

Violists have been constantly overlooked and underrated, and now we're ready to have our revenge. We have adapted their music for our own, we have written our own solos, we have taken their seats in orchestras, and we are gaining more converts all the time. And, as one violist said to his violinist and cellist colleagues, all viola jokes can be transposed up a fifth and down an octave. Don't get it? Ask a violist.

— Margaret Douglass

On Bathrooms

Institutional bathrooms are the antithesis of forests. By "forests," I specifically mean the verdant summer forests that cover the glacial moraines of Wisconsin; by "institutional bathrooms," I generally mean all those fluorescent-lighted, sterilized, steel-and-linoleum excretory morgues that infest malls, medical centers, and nearly every office building. Unless the bathrooms are in bookstores or arty restaurants, they almost never have anything on the walls; the materials used in their construction have invariably never lived; and the liquid soap never smells like anything — anything recognizable, natural, or pretty, at least.

The terror of the institutional bathroom is that its very mission is to reduce a life process that is by nature messy and stinky to an efficient and precise operation that leaves behind no evidence save a lightened bladder and a slight reduction in toilet paper. Institutional bathrooms change an art into a science. Each activity associated with pooping or peeing takes place in its own chamber: disrobing, excreting, disposing, cleaning, drying. The bathroom's visitor aims to touch as little as possible during his stay. There is never a connection with the bathroom; no experience in one should be memorable, if the bathroom functions as planned.

By contrast, every excretion in the woods is an adventure: Will bugs crawl into sensitive areas? Will the leaves nearby be sufficiently large for cleanup? Is anyone — or anything — watching?

To poop in the woods is to contribute to a vital, thriving

ecosystem in the tradition of my ancestors. I poop; deer poop. Bears shit in the woods. Leaving behind my own droppings gives me a sense of community with the natural world; whatever my pretensions to civilization and sophistication might be, I'm in line with the birds and bees when I'm dropping a load. And, my business done, I leave my mark: a feast for bugs that will soon decompose into the most fecund of soils. Happy plants will sprout from my beautiful gift to the world.

It's shameful, however, to be caught in a stark and lifeless institutional bathroom. Strangers in bathrooms never meet; when those who know each other share a bathroom, a curt acknowledgment is usually the extent of their interaction. Farts are still taboo; stays should be brief; liquids must be aimed meticulously and uncreatively. Bathrooms and their anonymous designers discourage innovation by users.

In our world, our central role is to be consumers. But in bathrooms, we don't consume — we create. Maybe that's why malls and insurance offices seem so uncomfortable with them. If we're not spending money, the malls try to hustle us in and out as quickly as possible. All evidence of our creative power is whisked away — by flushing toilets, drains, garbage cans. With motion detectors on sinks, urinals, and stalls, and with air dryers instead of paper towels, we're robbed of the sensual sensations that make excreting so interesting. White walls, white floors, white porcelain, and white lights drain the color from our products and from our faces in the mirror. The rest of the mall is infused with color, music, and smells, each enticing us to a new purchasable delight; shirts, CDs, and cookies beckon. In the bathroom, we're reminded to wash our hands thoroughly.

Though living in houses takes away our chance to excrete in nature, we still give life to our bathrooms. We make them as human as we can: Toothbrushes remind us that we eat sugar (and perhaps drink coffee or smoke), books remind us that we think and speak, molded soaps remind us that we get dirty and that we can enjoy getting clean. A squeezable bottle of sunblock might highlight our sometimes dangerous love of real warmth and light; a thick terry-cloth bathrobe might evoke rich thoughts of languid showers and breakfasts with newspapers. A bathroom in a house is not a wild adventure or a silent, mechanical terror — it's home.

So with institutional bathrooms at one extreme and the woods at the other, humans, typically, create a space in between. We love to venture into the forest, explore our metaphysical roots, perhaps examine literal roots as we squat and strain a few feet away. But if pooping in the woods is our history, institutional bathrooms don't have to be our future. Devoid of sights, sounds, smells, tastes, and textures, their antiseptic efficiency is out of tune with who we are. So, bathroom designers: Put some weird posters on the wall. Put some music on a boom box next to the sink. Let us use bars of hand soap that smell like roses. Maybe a few more people would catch a bug for want of 100% sterile hand detergents, but so what? Personally, I'd rather have a vivid, natural sniffle than the subtle, indistinct, impersonal sickness that comes from being treated as a biological machine rather than as a human.

I hate that kind of crap.

— Benjamin Wikler

Aubade to childhood

[one]
something tells me Shakespeare
would never have gone by "Billy."

the name commands very little from adulthood
rolling as it does in small balanced somersaults.

[two]
from years away
I hear children playing in the road
unscathed by the passing traffic
hitting tennis balls with aluminum bats
sending them orbiting off over foreign ground
over the neighbor's roof.

first, a bent ash
second, some collapsed hubcap
third, a stolen fluorescent cone
(it took three of us to carry it from the ditch).
I tagged each base as my brothers ran off
to find our ball on the other side of our world
and as the gravel spit itself
from under my running feet,
I hear them all calling my name out.

"Billy . . . Billy . . . Billy!"
I believed I could keep circling forever.

[three]

my little sister is making a man
of our lawn, shaving it too close
and letting the dry soil cloud like the Midwest,
though we are far from there now.

in sixth grade
I stole my brother's razor and pretended
to grow up. face to face to the mirror,
I trained my hand
to glide the razor against my smooth skin
with the grace of the lawnmower
disturbing the surface of the yard
but resolving nothing.

and I would have gotten away with it
but in the finishing moments
I grew impatient, drew my head and chin back
to nick my youthful skin.
it stung at first. then the blood
swelled against the lather
as if to boast at its escape.

and I rinsed my minor wound, cleaning nothing,
then ran from the bathroom to hide my face in a towel
until dinner.

[four]

people ask me and I answer.

nothing is wrong with "William,"
perched on the line like a hungry bird.
but everything becomes devoured by maturity.

something dies and is buried
in the empty lot — a young bird —
and quiet comes to an empty house.
children play ball there
and curse over the sacred ground.

the other birds, amazed by the strange
displacement of a generation,
call to the children to come back outside
and play again under the estranged sun.

nothing is wrong with "William,"
I tell them, but why do things have to change?

[five]

I once attempted to learn cursive
a tangle of loops and circles. I finished,
unsuccessful, and waited, misplaced
among the settled rows of desks
for the teacher to come with her ruler.

maybe, I decide, I have remained
attached to my young name
because I would hate to have to learn another,
afraid of that illegible language of children.

[six]

December was the shortest it has ever been
and the warmest. I remember
what we call "snow" in Florida,
though it melts impatiently as it falls earthward.

To celebrate, I did not rejoice in Christ's honor,
instead struggled to reconnect
to the visions of sugarplums I no longer dream of.
I spied from second-story mall railings
not on Santa, but on the children who worship him
then dart off like wild pigeons
still clinging to their mothers and fathers.

Christmas day, I too clung to my father.

He unwrapped more toys than I did
and I helped him test them,
drove down to a 7-11
to check the reception on long-distance
walkie-talkies. "Red Dog One to Blue Fox Three."
He came in loud and clear.

[finis]

The dawn is up. We wait at the dockside
since midnight. My 18th, threshold
of nothing really, but cigarettes and lottery tickets,
neither of which I celebrate,
and instead of parading down the lapped shore,
tightfisted and unruly, I have been calling my name out
to the water's edge for hours,
begging my youth to remain attached
to my branches like unripe fruit.
I hope I listen.

— William Merrell

In Ohio There Are No Whales

I knew this girl once. She was tall, and very thin, and my mother said she could stand a few pans of lasagna, then she'd be fine. Yes sir, a few pans, she said, that'd do it.

Her name was Lindsay but I never called her that, because in reality she didn't want to be her name. So I called her Daphne, for a reason I don't remember and isn't important.

She said to me one day, Let's go see the whales at the aquarium.

Why? I asked.

Because I've lived in this city for seventeen years and I've just now realized how special it is that we have whales. I mean, do you know how many cities have whales in them?

Live whales? I asked.

Yes, she said. Live whales.

No, I said. How many?

Twenty, she said. Twenty cities.

Twenty exactly? I asked.

Yes, she said. Twenty exactly.

That's not that many, I said.

Bingo, she said.

I met her at the aquarium right by the manatees or the sharks — one of the two, I'm not sure which. They were swimming around in water. That much I remember.

You have a hard time finding the place? she asked.

No, I said. I live five minutes away from here. Remember?

Oh yeah, she said. I forgot.

The whales were at the east end of the aquarium. We were at the west end, since that was where the parking lot was.

Do you want to see the whales now? I asked.

We'll get there, she said. We'll make our way to them eventually. The place isn't that big.

Yeah, I said. It could be bigger.

We walked past dolphins over which little kids made a big deal and adults commented on how intelligent they were. The dolphins, that is. An aquarium employee in khaki shorts and a navy blue short-sleeved polo shirt with an emblem on it told the gathering of folks what the names of these little wonders were.

Their names were Eddie and Rowena.

Aren't they amazing, folks? he asked. He was not yet out of that part of his life where he got horrible acne. His hair was cut in an ugly way and his voice made me feel light-headed. Daphne turned towards me.

Doesn't his voice make you nauseous? she asked, and crinkled her long, thin nose and squinted her coral eyes.

Yeah, I said. Let's get out of here.

But she hung around for a minute and twenty-six seconds, watching. Not Eddie and Rowena, but this guy talking about them. He was shorter than she was — she was almost as tall as me — and he had a stomach that was not yet completely devoid of baby fat and maybe never would be. His arms and legs were thin and not at all muscular.

I touched her left elbow. She looked down at it, at the middle and index finger on my right hand barely reaching the outermost tip of the round bone protruding from her arm. Her hair was short and reflected the soft sun of the day as she tilted her head down. After a while she looked up at me.

Isn't that sad? she asked.

What?

Isn't it?

What?

Let's go. I don't want to see the dolphins anymore, she said.

We walked toward the sharks. Yeah, it was the sharks, so the ones before must've been manatees. Or something.

I talked to Eric yesterday, she told me.

Eric? I asked. You mean over the phone or in an e-mail or what?

On the phone.

Wow. That's the first time in a while.

Yeah. We haven't done that for a long time.

How long exactly?

Eight months.

Wow.

Yeah.

Did he call you or did you call him?

I called him. I got sick of it.

He was home?

Yeah, I know. It's amazing that he was home, isn't it? I mean, how long has it been since that's happened?

Did his parents pick up first?

No, it was him right away.

Wow. Usually you talk to his parents first.

Yeah, I talk to them a lot.

You know them better than you do him, I joked, which I thought I shouldn't have done right after I did it.

She gave a short laugh. Yeah, she said, I've gotten to know them pretty well.

What did he say?

Different things. He's changed over the summer, you know.

Yeah.

Sort of like you have.

I have?

Yeah, you have.

I don't think so.

You don't know it.

I think I'd know.

No, you wouldn't know. You never know.

You never know, I repeated. I wonder why not.

He's still with Caitlyn.

Wow. They've been together for a while now, haven't they?

Yeah, well, he loves her, I guess.

I guess.

We got to the sharks. They swam in a jerky way, moving in short spurts in different directions, sometimes at us, sometimes not. Their tank was huge and lit from inside so the glass we saw them through was glowing just a little bit, reflecting off of our faces. I looked at her and her face was shiny, her eyes were white more than blue, her lips looked like they were glistening with something wet.

A light gray shark came right at us and snapped his huge mouth and this six- or seven- or eight-year-old next to me jumped back just a little bit into his father. The father moved his hand down to the boy's shoulder, then used the hand to push his son's head farther into his blue-jeaned hip.

The whales are two sections away, I told her. She wasn't blinking anymore as she stared as the sharks.

Yeah, she said, looking away after a while. Let's go.

We walked a little on the cheap burgundy carpet of the aquarium that was a little wet, though I couldn't figure why, since everything was in a tank, and the tanks looked pretty solid to me.

He ever tell you that? I asked.

What? she asked.

You know.

What?

That he loved you.

Yeah. Better than that, actually.

When?

A while ago.

Eight months ago?

No, a little bit before that. Around Christmas, actually.

He told you he loved you?

Yeah.

Why?

What?

Why did he tell you that?

Why did he tell me that he loved me?

Yeah.

Why are you asking me that?

What?

Why are you asking me that?

I'm wondering.

How am I supposed to know?

What's better than that?

Better than what?

Better than telling you he loved you.

What?

What part of Ohio is he from again?

She said some town that was near some city in Ohio here, but I don't remember what either of them were.

Oh, I said.

Yeah, she said.

Any aquariums there? I asked.

In Ohio?

Yeah. In Ohio. It's possible, right?

No. No aquariums there.

So no whales, I guess, huh?

I think it'd be kind of hard, what with no aquariums and all.

Yeah, I guess so.

Where are they? she asked all of a sudden, stopping.

I took a few more steps and then realized she'd stopped, then stopped myself and turned back towards her. What? I asked.

Where are they?

Who? What?

The whales.

I turned back around, saw a sign that pointed around a corner, and said, "Whales." She followed my eyes, saw where I was looking.

Come on, I said. We'll go see the whales. I started to walk towards the corner.

She wasn't following. No, she said. I don't want to see the whales.

What? I asked. I stopped.

I don't want to, she said.

That's why we came.

I know.

But you don't want to see them?

No. I don't want to see them.

I looked at her, felt a cold gust of wind pass over my face because now we were outside, since the area where the whales were had to be outside.

What do you want to do? I asked.

What?

What do we do now? I asked. If we're not seeing the whales, I mean.

Let's go home, she said.

And miss the whales? I asked. Are you sure?

Yeah, she said. I don't want to see the whales today.

— Matthew Fitting

Occident Meets Orient

"Hello? Mrs. Li?" the voice on the phone says.

"Uh, yes, this is she," I hesitantly reply. I hate lying, but sometimes one must do it.

"Hi. My name is Michelle, and I'm calling from AT&T. . . ."

I have answered millions of calls like this one, and each time I have to lie that I am Mrs. Li. I know lying is a sin, but dying of embarrassment is worse. My parents, after all these years, still cannot speak or understand English very well. They can handle the normal "Hi, how ah you? Fine, thanks" and "I'd like to cash these checks, please," but they cannot carry on a conversation for longer than thirty seconds after they run out of those lines taught in the *Traveler's Handbook — 1000 English Phrases to Use.* So when a company calls to advertise, I end up answering the call and pretending that I am "the lady of the house." Sometimes, my mom is daring enough to answer a call, but I snatch the phone out of her hand for fear that she will accidentally order two thousand dollars' worth of replacement windows, or switch long-distance phone companies.

I am especially afraid of phone calls from teachers. My teachers never call my house, but one of my brother's teachers did during his freshman year because he wanted to tell my parents that my brother was doing very well. One night after dinner the phone rang while I was absorbed in my chemistry assignment. I picked up the phone and casually answered, "Hello?"

"Hi, can I speak to Mr. or Mrs. Li, please?"

"Um, can I ask who's calling, please?"

"Yes, this is Mr. Boyle from the high school. I am Steve's math teacher."

Oh great, I thought to myself. I did not want to lie to a teacher, but I did not want to tell him that my parents could not speak English. Not wanting to hurt my pride, I took a deep breath and said, "This is Mrs. Li." Each time I identify myself as Mrs. Li, I worry that I may be caught lying, but I cannot bring myself to tell others that my parents cannot speak English, either. So lying is my only option.

Lying on the phone has not gotten any easier for me over the years, but it is better than having to face this dilemma in public. A lot of teens dread being with their parents in front of their friends for fear that they may say something stupid, but my problem is the opposite. My parents, insisting that Americans speak way too fast, can never fully grasp what my friends' parents are trying to say to them, and therefore all they do is nod. For instance, once at a symphony concert my family bumped into my friend Alison's family. We have known each other for years, and our parents have seen one another many times. My dad, always the polite one in the family, stretched out his hand and said to Mr. Downton, "Hello. Nice to meet you." I was about to die. Then Mr. Downton, as my parents later told me, began to say, "Gilli gullu gilli gullu." My parents nodded as Mr. Downton spoke. I could not bear to watch, so Alison and I slipped away, leaving our parents to carry on a one-sided, dead-end conversation.

I was so embarrassed and furious. Why couldn't my parents just learn English? They tell me that they try, but sometimes I wonder if they are actually trying. Many Chinese Americans refuse to learn English because they say it is "gue lo" language — the ghosts' language. Maybe my parents do not want to learn English. After all, they only converse with Chinese people. They read Chinese newspapers. The only things missing are a Chinese TV station and a radio channel. *I have just about had enough of this nonsense*, I thought to myself. "Why can't you learn English?" I bluntly asked my parents as we were heading home.

My dad looked into the rearview mirror and said in Cantonese, "We are trying. You won't let us."

I could not believe it. My parents were blaming *me* for their inability to speak English! I turned to my brother, who was now laughing hysterically, and asked, "What's so funny?"

"Mr. Downton asked them a question, and all they said was 'yesnoyesnoyesno.'" He laughed even more hysterically.

I wanted to jump out of the car. I thought I would go insane if I did not. My parents could not speak English, and they blamed it on me. At that moment, I vowed to never show up with them again anywhere in public.

The timing could not have been better. I got my license soon after that incident. I no longer had to worry about my non-English-speaking parents following me around. I thought not having my parents around me would solve the problem, but I could not have been more wrong.

When my picture and my interview with the reporter was published in the *Cincinnati Enquirer* for winning the *USA Weekend* National Student Fiction Contest last May, my parents were ecstatic. They got out the Lexicome (our family's electronic Chinese-English dictionary) and read the article, looking up each word they did not know. I was mortified. Here I was, a nationally recognized young fiction writer, seeing her parents having to look up the words she spoke in a newspaper interview. My pride was shattered. I never read my own article, nor did I want to; it only served as a bitter reminder that my parents could not speak English like I wanted them to. My parents, thinking that I was just embarrassed by my picture, framed the article and called for a celebration. I simply refused, saying that I was busy. I did not want to set myself up for more embarrassment at the restaurant where I would have to order food for my parents because they could not do it themselves.

I spent that night, which should have been a night of celebrating my accomplishment, alone in my room, thinking about my parents' failure. My dad then knocked on my door and asked to come in.

"Ah Wai, I read your story, and I understand most of it," Daddy said (in Cantonese, of course). He understood most of it? That was a shock to me. He did not give me time to snap back at him, and he continued, "I know what you are trying to say. I know you are different from me. We are brought up in different cultures. But I don't want you to be ashamed of me and Mommy because we can't speak perfect English. Our parents were too poor to send us to college." Oh great, here comes the I-had-to-walk-seven-miles-to-school-each-day-in-canvas-shoes talk, I thought. He went on and said, "As a boy, I wanted to come to America to study. All my friends left for Australia, America, and Canada, and I was left in Hong Kong. Your grandpa couldn't afford any more education beyond high

51

school. Your mom and I were lucky to even earn a high school diploma. We don't want our children to go through the same thing we did, and so we brought you and Steve to America. I do know English. How else can I communicate with my American clients? If I were afraid to speak English, I wouldn't have any business. And what's the money for, anyway? It's for you to go to college. Your ma and I will send you to Hafoo (Harvard) and Yale-a (Yale) or anywhere you want to go. We just don't want you to be ashamed of us."

I did not say anything after Daddy made the speech. I was ashamed of myself for thinking that my parents were failures. Although I was still somewhat frustrated with the fact that they could not speak perfect English, I was beginning to appreciate their effort of trying their best.

The following day, I suggested that the family go out for dim sum. My parents were glad, probably even surprised, that I had made that suggestion. The four of us went together as a family, and we ate and chatted away in Cantonese at the restaurant.

— Silvia Li

This July Morning

I watch my grandfather,
one of three tenors in a Baptist choir.
"The Old Rugged Cross"
echoes through the loft,
but from his lips there is no sound,
from his tongue, no words.
He used to drown out every voice,
stretch for notes until he dripped with sweat,
but now he shivers when the room is hot,
and silence replaces crowns and crosses.

Today his tenor voice is missing.
My grandfather studies the page,
an Egyptian code he cannot break.
His shoulders hang, his eyebrows bunch
in frustration like a child learning to read.
He'll never know how closely I watch him,
how I cry to a cross of suffering and shame
that his memory will not fail him
when the music ends,
and he must remember my name.

— Darian Duckworth

Fifth Gear

"I was young once too, you know."
she watched her voice offer itself to the 11:15 blackness,
reviewing hints from the *Good Housekeeping* article,
"Times your teen will open up to you"
> *"When you are in the car, there are no distractions,*
> *and you don't have to make eye contact,"*
She was paying more attention
to the men in the eighteen-wheelers
she was passing in fifth gear than to her mother,
but maybe the next tip would help,
> *"Late at night, when they're worn out,*
> *and they've let their defenses down,"*
She could see her daughter's dark eyes
glistening in the waxing moon outside the cracked windshield.
Crying, she'd be more vulnerable and open,
the article promised. If not,
> *"You open up first,"*
So she fingered her zipper,
"I have had my heart broken too,
The first time was in junior high,"
but she couldn't tell her daughter he'd sent her a preprinted valentine,
had only given his sloppy signature to her,
and she'd fallen for him.
Couldn't tell her now her heart did a double-dutch
when her brother teased, taffy sticky on his lips,
"Mary Emma, it's a *boy* for you,"

And she'd skip to the one telephone,
in the middle of her father reading the evening newspaper,
her mother cooking dinner for twelve,
and all nine curious, jealous sisters and brothers
hurried down the stairs, huddled around her.
Couldn't tell how one June day he held Susan Sotheby's hand
(her father owned the town department store),
and she'd run home in her Mary Janes and plaid pleated Catholic girl skirt,
past the phone by the banister,
up the worn stairs,
and locked herself in the bedroom she shared with three sisters.
Her daughter would probably laugh.

— Kelly Davison

Sea Salt

I never saw the beach until I was six and my sister Nicole was twelve. Our mother wouldn't allow us to go in the water. "You girls know what happened to Timmy Bird," she said, and tightened her face.

"Yes, Mom." We'd heard the story before. Our mother and her youth group went to the beach with fifteen other children. They spent the entire day on the island, and only waded in the water up to their knees. Still, little Timmy Bird stepped in a hole, and no one saw him slip under until he was too far out and our mother saw him kick and stretch from the water's belly. His small white legs were bruised like bananas. "And we fifteen kids had to hold hands and wade through the water to look for him." I could see my mother lifting her body out of the sea, as though each step stole energy to move her limbs, as though she was searching through glue. "The water darkened that day," she told us.

Nicole and I heard the story so many times we could recite it with our mother's same worried look. We mastered deepening our eyes, and the sincere promise of staying away from the sea. Nicole was better at this than me.

In August we packed more than a week's worth of things, and our mother rented a minivan to hold our bikes and bags of crossword-puzzle and word-search books. They banged against the back door each time she took a sharp turn on the way to North Carolina. My sister discovered the puzzles her fourth-grade year at a gas station, and now she planned on counting them as her summer reading. She was in the red section labeled "Advanced," with four-syllable and archaic words.

Mother let us stop at the Dollar Store, which always smelled of cheap raspberry-peach air fresheners and candles. The scent cut my throat dead center like a dartboard and made me gag until I'd been inside for a while and had adjusted to the thick, fruity air. We picked up bubble gum and generic brands of soda pop, with names like Doc Terrific and Lemon-Lime Burst. They sold sunglasses at the Dollar Store, too. I found a pair with purple frames.

"They make you look like a bug," my sister said. I was too short to see in the mirror, but I liked them anyway because everything looked green, and Nicole was a large dancing cucumber, Martian, or willow tree. Mom told us to hurry if we wanted to be at the hotel before lunch.

"You look like Janis Joplin, Terry." Mom said it with affection, and I didn't know which of Mom's friends was Janis, but I liked her.

Our mother thought it would be fun to blindfold us before we reached the shore. She gave my sister a blue bandanna. Nicole cheated, I was sure. She looked at her feet, which she never does, her shoulders slumped, and her head bent down into her neck like the big white birds we saw on the marsh before we got here. My sister never looked at her shoes; she was afraid she'd miss something. I got to wear my mother's scarf, although I never knew she wore them, this must have been something new. The scarf reminded me of Grandma, but it smelled like Mom. It had too many flowers. There was a big chaotic mess of them, pinks and greens appeared to have had a fight, a violent spitting up of oranges and overgrown leaves. The scarf was long and brushed my back when I walked, as though I had long hair. Mom promised that when we got to the beach she'd make us shell barrettes for our hair. Nicole and I never had those, always leaving our hair down and straight. The other girls in our classes had lots of barrettes, some they made themselves with puff paint and neon shoelaces. Others had barrettes with the days of the week, their names, or a favorite color, but we left our hair down. Mom even bought a hot-glue gun, and it appeared that we were molding into other families who had crafty moms, who spent their Saturdays making T-shirts and pot holders.

We held Mom's hands. Nicole complained that she didn't need to hold anyone's hand, that she'd finished the sixth grade. Together, we were a loud clatter of flip-flops. We walked down the dock steps and felt what I thought was sand on my toes, and I wondered if my sister could see it. I wondered if it looked like it did in books. Spice. Sugar or salt. Cinnamon or cumin.

"We're here, girls," Mom said, looking at me, like something she'd rehearsed or planned to say. Immediately, Nicole pushed her bandanna down. She was a bandit from out West, with her neck and lower lip partially hidden and her words muffled like an old man's. "Look at the water!" I'd already taken my sandals off; I found myself sinking down so that the sand rose above my ankles.

Nicole laughed. "You look handicapped, Terry. Like you don't have any feet!" She carried my buckets and sand toys.

They used to be Nicole's, with her initials all over them in big red marker. Some were written in my mother's handwriting. The others I assumed were Nicole's, with backward N's and cutesy starred i's.

My mother held an umbrella and cooler in her arms. The umbrella was mine, because I didn't tan like my mom and sister, and even though I'd never had a sunburn that I could remember (except on my nose), I'd seen pictures of my dad with a burn, and my mother told me I didn't want one.

We dropped our things far away from the water. My sister began to strip like no one was watching. She had developed this new habit the previous week in Sunday school, when we were informed that God saw everything. For days she changed in the closet with her back facing the door until she realized that He saw her there, too, and then she didn't care. Nicole was the only one in our family with an outie belly button, and from certain angles it stuck out farther than her nose.

"Race you to the water," she said. I agreed, knowing she'd win, and started. My sister was a seagull then, with thin legs and stiff movements. She was loud. The wind blew.

"Only to your ankles," our mother called out, but we already knew. I missed Mom's scarf, the fake hair that tickled my bones.

"I hate this sand. Whenever the wind blows it stings my legs." Nicole hunched over and rubbed her knees. She bent so far I could see down her bathing suit. Her chest was rulered in brown-and-white lines. She shaved her legs just to come on the trip, and declared herself a woman. She was going into the seventh grade.

Since our summer vacation, our mother decided to make

trips to the coast every time something eventful occurred in our lives. She claimed to have missed the sea, although sometimes I saw her wince on our walks down the beach.

"Are you okay, Mom? Did you step on a shell or something?"

"No, honey, I'm fine." I thought maybe Dad was in the air, the way she took in huge gulps of the wind while she cried. She hadn't seen the beach since our father left, and in the short week I could see a new piece of her — a younger woman had grown into a sister or daughter. These trips began to last longer than a few weeks; we brought more things. We even owned our own minivan. This seemed silly to me, because minivans were meant for large families, and there were only three of us. We got one anyway; my mother was conforming and wanted to sign us up for soccer. We hated sports.

Even our town began to fail; it had been perfect for six years but somehow lost it. She knew it too well and found herself in too many gas stations, giving too many directions, to places she'd been too many times. Now she was talking with a real estate agent about moving. Our grandmother was not that far from a house she was looking at. If we moved, Mom wouldn't have to pay for after-school care anymore, and our mother always liked a good deal. We would have moved sooner, but Mom was still hesitant about bringing us closer to the water.

I was beginning to like the new minivan and even staked claims for the backseat. I liked it because I could keep watch on everyone, and it was my own seat back there, sectioned off and small. When we went to the grocery store Mom put the plastic bags in my seat and the trunk. She told me to sit with my sister, but I made room, cradling the egg cartons in my arms, keeping the milk flush against my thighs. Our house was too far away from the grocery store to go every day like our father liked to do. We had things in the pantry, of course, but he liked to shop for the meal. He stopped by on his way home from work for fancy things like water chestnuts and bell peppers. Mom couldn't do that, so she brought us with her, with promises of candy bars and magazines at the checkout line. She pulled into the space, and I could only see a rectangle of Mom's face in the rearview mirror. I thought she was looking at me but she wasn't. I turned around and there was a father pushing an overstuffed cart, squeaky wheels vibrating over the pavement. He had three kids, and I couldn't clearly see their faces. They were blurred behind the tinted windows. Mom gripped the steering wheel tighter. Her rings seemed to bulge off her hands.

"Girls?" She tried to keep her voice level. We didn't respond, just looked at her, and I whipped my head around to make sure she didn't notice I saw what she was looking at. "Who's up for KFC? You girls didn't really feel up to going shopping today, did you?" Before we had a chance to answer, Mom was already pulling out of her parking space. She didn't even look, and I don't think she would have cared if she hit the man or his wife, the little children who were stuck to the grocery cart like monkeys. I pushed my face into the window. A print of my cheek and nose winked back at me, and the little boy waved and stuck out his tongue. I reminded myself to look for him on my first day of school.

I missed dinners with our father, maybe even more than

Nicole. Mom never went back to the grocery store. She made little lists for Grandma to get, and somehow we were never around when the groceries came. The food filled up the house late at night I imagined, like Christmas. We spent more meals with Grandma. She let us hang out in the kitchen before we even sat down for breakfast. She snuck us strips of bacon as if we were little clicking dogs at her heels. Our mother never cooked. She ritually bought potato salad, vegetables, and already-roasted chicken, and she laid them on the table and left the room. Sometimes she stayed and said grace with us. Mom held my hand so tight I thought it would fall off, and I wondered how tight she held Nicole's, but I never asked her. It wasn't until we moved to the beach that I knew what Mom's hands felt like. Dad always held Nicole's and mine for the blessing. We were divided. At dinner I tried to pretend what it would be like if Dad was still there. I could still see my sister when she ate; they concentrated on each bite, rolled their eyes in the back of their heads, and answered each other's questions about the day with a mouthful of food. Nicole turned over the fork to look at a bite from all angles. The two concentrated on each other, and I was left to talk to my mother, who frequently asked me to pass the salt, and that was it. Mom began to touch me, my shoulders, back, and hair, and she said my name when she addressed me. My sister has noticed this, too, I think, and she touched her own hair and said Mom's name. She ate differently in our new home. I told her she should be an artist for colors she can make out of our meals, but when she wasn't an artist, my sister was a bird.

Some days my sister was younger than me. She sat in the

back of the car, and I took her seat on Saturday errands with Mom. I kept checking on her in the rearview mirror, but my sister was almost dead. She was chapped lips and hiccups. "You girls need to get out of these slumps," my mother said as she lowered the volume on the radio. She stopped the car and forced us to get out. We were only five minutes from home, but she stopped anyway. "C'mon," she said, and it was something in her voice that made Nicole willingly unbuckle her seat belt. Mom had two empty water bottles and gave us each one. "Go for it," she said.

"Huh?" We didn't understand.

"Go to the water and fill up your bottles and come back," she said. "And hurry." We were afraid at first but went down to the shore and filled our bottles, holding them underwater for a long time, watching the bubbles pop up until they were full to the rim. We brought them back. "Good," she said. "We're making sea salts tonight."

For days my sister and I checked on our water bottles. We prayed that the water would fly away and leave the crusted salt, leave the entire bottle full of it. We were surprised to find it harder and not as white as table salt. Mom ran a bath for us and dunked us in. We watched as the salt we worked so hard to form disappeared into the water. The water stung for a minute, but it was better than any bubble bath I'd ever taken.

"It gets all the impurities out," Mom said. "You'll be as shiny as new pennies." When we were out of the bath, I could have sworn I heard Mom splashing her toes around. She must have been getting her feet wet.

Our new home didn't have an air conditioner. It was hot,

and my sister and I fought for the bathroom floor. The tile kept our salty skin cool. We were little shrimp over ice. We lay naked in the bathtub or on linoleum; the bathtub kept us cooler. Occasionally, the faucet dripped and pricked our toes. It sent pings of chill surging through our veins like power lines. It kept me comfortable but awake. My sister was on her back on the floor. She was a rainbow fish. She no longer had visible blood to pinken her face or chest. Her eyes somersaulted underneath the skin and flickered like lightning bugs.

Her T-shirt was inside out on the commode and her shoes were beside me. I could smell them, the sulfur and fish scent that the entire house could smell like at times. The scent someone might imagine the house smelling of from just looking at the outside, with the fishing poles propped up against the frames like they didn't have the strength to stand. They were there for appearance, to fit the mood of the home. No one in our family fished. They were our father's old poles, and he didn't need them anymore, or maybe he just forgot.

I was ready to throw the foul-smelling shoes across the room or at Nicole when I saw a photograph that had slipped to the heel of her sneakers. It was our father. It was a picture of him on the boat, our old boat that I never saw — the boat my sister used to tell me about at night. She stayed up and climbed into my bed, her pajama collar soaked, and she drooled stories all over me, leaked water and sand, boats and tales of our mother in love. She oozed every bit of her life that I was not a part of into me. She drained Mom's hatred at not having a family through my skin and began to feel better. Only then was my sister real and I could feel our father and see him leave, see our mother cry over her beautiful little family that was shattering like bitter shells.

"What are you doing with this?" Nicole's eyes opened wide — she hadn't been asleep. She sat up and scrambled toward me on all fours.

"Give me that!" she said. I retrieved it and held it behind my back.

"Where did you get this?" We weren't allowed to have pictures of him. I knew it was our dad, the way the skin on his forehead and cheeks looked tough, and Nicole was in his lap. I sounded like my mother for the way I snapped at my sister, and was afraid for Nicole, the way she still knew him, thought about him, and held on to him. She wasn't like Mom, who drowned him the day he sailed to sea. That night Nicole promised to share the photograph with me if I prayed to the moon, hoping the tide would bring him back so he'd toss up onto the shore at night like the prettiest untouched shell and uncracked bottles, filled with what made our skin the cleanest.

— Jennifer Hall

My Mother Tells the Story of Her Alabama Childhood

When I was a child we were white we were not white
because we loved it wanted it worshiped it We were white
because we were afraid, we wanted to be left alone
We were white because we needed work we needed
a way to live we wanted a chance — so we were white.
All the teachers were white I hated them I hated
their sour breath crooked teeth false smiles frizzy hair
They liked the sly dough-faced girls with blonde curls
whose parents sent candy at Christmas
I hated those girls I hated the country boys with sharp
weasel faces who called me half-breed, redskin,
shoved me when no one was looking but I didn't tell.
I put up with it I didn't let on I cared
because silence was the price of being white.
My grandmother was not white she was brown,
she was a Creek Indian old sweet she smelled of lavender
One summer day when I was twelve she took me to town
in the drugstore there were tables for white people
I sat down but she had to stand at the end of the counter.
The pimply-faced soda jerk smirked but he stopped
when he saw how straight and proud my Grandma stood
There were girls from school whispering giggling
they were white they would grow up to be
just like their mothers — wear bright red lipstick,
shorts and halters with high heels sleep with the neighbor

My grandmother stood quiet in her blue-flowered
dress and old lady shoes she was tall and brown
like a great live oak with all-embracing arms,
with roots going down, down so they find water
other trees can't find and they live for centuries
the light from the doorway fell on her white hair
I thought I love you I want to be like you I want to be
what you are I stood and walked toward my grandmother
her eyes said do you know what you're doing
there's no going back my eyes said Yes
There was silence no one looked at us
the clerk dropped his eyes and turned away
the girls stopped giggling stared at the table
and stirred their milkshakes with their straws
I stood beside my grandmother waiting for fear
that did not come and after that day
I was never white again.

— Elisabeth Gorey

Untouchable Names

Dear Um-mah,

I was never Sarah to you, but Ji-In. Those two syllables carry a thousand meanings hidden in centuries of scholarly brushes that stroked rice paper against a background of Arirang music. I remember you told me those meanings once. But I've forgotten, and I'd rather forget. And then, perhaps when I reach the age of forty-five, I'll ask again, checking to see if I've fulfilled the blessings bestowed upon me at birth. I'd rather not know till then, Um-mah.

My nursery school teachers never could pronounce my name right. "Ji-*In*." They would curl their lips into ridiculous Os, never mastering the soft "g" accented with a slight "ch" sound. Their lips, painted an '80s pink, were always admirable in their ability to stick together and part in waves that receded slowly in opposite directions to the corners of their mouths. Here, they would magically disappear.

My name did the same as it receded into "Sarah" when I entered kindergarten. The oh-so-hard-to-pronounce level of schooling, was it not? I, Sarah Chang, now knew we meant business. I was now open to customers twenty-four hours a day, seven days a week. I now had a gender. But you and Dad would remain hermaphrodites for all time, "*J*ung S*e*uk and *J*in Kon — now, dear — which one is your mother?" I should've said both, Um-mah. I wonder what that would've done to her perfectly painted lips.

In the soybean-colored texture of blanketing you melt into time frames of a child — at least in my eyes. To me you were never that grass-blade girl enclosed in delicate black and white, so thin that neighbors used to say a slight summer breeze would carry you away. Was it summer, Um-mah, when you boarded that plane? When Hawaiian leis were wrapped around your milk-white neck? It was then, when sweet seaweed and Great-aunt's perfume filled your pale nostrils, that your name un-leashed the summer breeze that blew you away across the Pacific.

Your name, Mi-Jin, was a name that other brothers, sisters, Mother, and Father called you, for it echoed a childhood of narrow dirt lanes and pale-blue garden gates. Said in lilting tones of Korean voices, it carried in the wind and landed on your father's morning glories. Did your family know that they were sending a loved one away every time they called your name? "Mi" was to be beautiful, and "Jin" was one who would embark upon a great journey, free to go. Grandfather would joke and say that he had carefully chosen "Mi" to foretell the future, when his daughter would one day step upon American ("Mi"-Gook) soil and prosper.

So it sent you to the land of Mickey Mouse and McDonald's luxury, where kimchee breath was a rare joy. But that name was a one-way ticket, Um-mah. It contained one last syllable that remained forgotten in your parents' home of wood and fra-grance — "Kon." You stamped yourself on American paper as Jin Kon Chang, dropping the "Mi" and allowing "Kon" to come alive and hold you fast. "Kon" meant "earth" and bound you to this land.

You prefer "Mi-Jin," don't you, Um-mah? When jindo dogs ran loose in your backyard and you watched the cotton candy man spin his silky fabric? When afternoons were spent with captured butterflies, pinned down and displayed? When grasshoppers were roasted — there was no limit on this meal — and rice cakes smeared on fingers? Twenty years later, your daughter had Häagen-Dazs ice cream and french fries together, much to your disapproval. But as I shall never be Sarah to you, but Ji-In, to me you shall always remain beautiful and free — Mi-Jin.

Love,
Ji-In

— Sarah Chang

A Domestic Conversation

He was sitting by the table, staring out the window, when she entered the kitchen. For a moment, she looked at him, ridiculous in his ragged blue robe and uncombed hair, and wanted to roll her eyes. She didn't, though; he looked up at her all too soon, anxious to share his thoughts.

She turned to the dirty dishes lying on the counters and in the sink, not wanting to encourage him. It was maddening to hear him talk lately.

"Where have you been?"

She clanked dishes into the dishwasher. "Went to the grocery store. Then I was outside raking the leaves."

Where have you been? Maybe that was the question he wanted her to ask. *Why have you been in bed for half the day?* Maybe that was it; maybe that was the question he wanted to answer. But she wouldn't ask it. Not today. She was tired of his answers.

She opened the cabinet and looked at the containers to make sure she had what she needed to bake her chicken casserole tonight. Really, she could do this. She could go on with the day as she'd gone on with every other day before. It didn't matter if he wanted to sit around all day, looking out every window in the house, amazed at the greatness of his own thoughts. She could go on.

Unless he talked, that is.

"Marianne, do you ever wonder why we do this?"

She focused harder. It was the cloves she was looking for.

71

"Do what, Henry?" She succeeded in making herself sound as if she were talking to a child.

"All of this. Everything we do."

She left the cabinet open and found her recipe box on a shelf on the other side of the room. "I don't know, Henry. Maybe because we have a church social to go to tonight."

He looked at her and made that "don't play games with me" face that he had learned to use so aptly as a father. She was too busy thumbing through the recipe cards to take notice.

"You know that's not what I mean, Marianne."

She scanned the card quickly. There it was. The cream of mushroom soup. How could she have forgotten that? She walked behind Henry to the large cabinet that held the soup cans and opened the door to peer inside, hating to be so close to him.

"I'm tired of this, Marianne. I'm tired of church socials on weekends and work on weekdays. I'm tired of pretending it all means something, tired of people thinking that we know anything about anything."

Tired, Henry? Are you still "tired of work" after calling in sick every day this week, lying around like a dead dog? Are you tired of church because you sit in the back and let your arrogant eyes chastise everyone who tries to talk to you? You're tired, Henry? Well, we're tired of you. Tired of your life crisis and your "deep thoughts."

Cream of mushroom soup. There wasn't any. She'd have to go back down to the grocery store.

"Do you want me to call the church and tell them you aren't

coming?" She walked back to the other side of the room and closed the cabinet door.

"No, Marianne! That's ridiculous." He paused. "I just want you to talk with me."

She scrubbed the counter where the dirty dishes had left stains, trying to ignore the way she felt compelled to turn around and face him.

Finally, he broke the tension, turning his eyes away from her and back to the window. "Marianne, I just need to think about things. I need time to think over the things that I wouldn't think about otherwise. That's all."

There was one spot, a coffee stain that had been there for years, that drove her crazy. She pressed the washcloth into it, grinding back and forth furiously. She half muttered it: "It's taken you fifty years. . . ."

"Fifty years for what?" He didn't understand. Not for a second.

Fifty years, Henry, to see what you know when you're four years old. To see that the world is big, Henry.

"Fifty years to get tired of everything." It was a half-truth, at least.

He ignored it. "Marianne, they say even Einstein didn't know ninety-nine percent of the reasons for why things happen. He just explained what he saw. They'll tell you about atoms and forces and energy, but they really don't know anything, Marianne. Not anything."

She turned around and looked at her husband, throwing the dishcloth back into the sink. He was staring out the window again, consumed in the abstractness of his thoughts. *Don't talk to me about all that, Henry. I don't know anything about it. Do you know your granddaughter is thinking about having a baby, Henry? Can you feel that? Can you feel the four funerals we went to over the last ten years, the last days we saw each one of our parents? What's eighty years of life, Henry, and who cares? Who cares, Henry?*

"I have to go to the grocery store again. Do you need anything?" She went into the next room to get her coat and purse.

Henry got out of his chair and followed her. "What do you think, Marianne?"

She looked at him for a moment and then breezed past him, through the kitchen to the garage door. "I guess I don't understand it, Henry."

He came into the kitchen again, looking urgently at her. "Marianne —"

She cocked her head towards him, politely, apathetically obedient. "Yes?"

"When are you going to face yourself?"

She sighed, reaching for the keys on the wall and opening the door. "I'm going grocery shopping, Henry."

She shut the door behind her, letting its echo ring hollowly in the kitchen. There was nothing to say to him today, nothing that mattered more than the fact that she felt like she was choking, in his house and in his car.

— Dan Poston

Faking It

"Old jazz musicians never die. They just fake it."

— Anonymous

After sixty years of hitting wood and ivory, the pianist's hands were tired. They were tired and they were cumbersome; a pair of knock-kneed elephants trying to dance on their own tusks, twisting and gyrating clumsily until they fell exhausted into his lap. His music, too, had become cumbersome; the notes were heavy and humorless, each one more forced than the last. The pianist knew all this. He could feel his arthritic fingers strain, he knew that his music had become not a song but a scream. But he pretended to not know. He pretended to be oblivious and bent his head closer to the keys to hear the beauty that was no longer there.

The other musicians in the cabaret also knew that the pianist's hands were tired. During his solos, as he muscled out one clichéd line after another, they would catch each others' eyes across the stage. And when he took breaks, which were becoming more and more frequent, they would talk about him in whispers:

"He's gettin' old, man. His fingers's had it."

"Dude can't even play a good run no more. He lost his soul. Time for him to go. Someone ought t' say somethin'."

"We can't do that, man. Playin's his life. How you gone rob a man of his *life*? Won't be long now, 'fore he won't be able to make it down here no more, anyway. Then we can pull in someone else. You heard that new boy over in Louie's place? Dude's got some fire, man."

They repeated this conversation night after night, and the pianist, watching them from over his shoulder talk behind their hands, knew exactly what they were saying. He turned to the bar, ordered his drink, and started in on the girl sitting next to him. She was a pretty girl, about twenty. He rattled off a few of his better stories, and she giggled and moved a little closer to him.

He figured now was the time. "I'm a famous man, baby. A very famous man." He paused. "I look old to you? Some folks say I'm gettin' old. Guess they think I can't play. I remember Art Tatum, though, now there was an old dude, but nobody ever said he couldn't play, no, sir."

The girl giggled. "Who's Art Tatum?"

This conversation, too, was repeated every night, same conversation, different girl, who wouldn't know Art Tatum, or the Duke, or Count Basie, or Erroll Garner, and who would let him buy her a drink and who wouldn't stay after that. The girls never stayed anymore, really. The pianist noticed this, too, but he told himself that it was because the city was getting worse and the girls didn't want to stay out late now. So he would sit at the bar, swirling the dark bourbon absentmindedly, until one of the other guys walked up softly behind him, touched his elbow, said, "C'mon, man, time to go." And he would allow himself to be led out of the bar, put in a cab, and be driven away, nearly etherized, into the looming blankness of the city.

On this night, he sat silently in the back of the taxi, feeling more tired than usual, and he noticed that his hands were trembling with age, that he couldn't hold them still, even for a second. Flitter. Flitter. The cab rolled through the streets, bumping along on a road made of old beer bottles, finally pulling up in front of the pianist's apartment. A moving truck hulked silently on the curb outside.

The pianist opened the door, stuck a rubbery leg on the ground. "Thanks, my man," he said to the driver, and moved to get out. "Say, if you like jazz, you should come hear me and my boys sometime. Right where you picked me up, down there in the old quarter."

The driver shifted. "*No comprende*," he said. "Fiftee' dolla'."

When the cab had pulled away, the pianist staggered up his steps, alone and slightly drunk. There was a note tacked to his door. "Furniture repossessed," it said, "as payment for debts. Balance due: $980.67. Signed, R. S. Morgan, prop., Morgan and Sons, Repossessors."

The pianist shook his head and fumbled for his keys, muttering under his breath, "Loada crap. Bill Evans never had his furniture repossessed, bet. Monk, neither. They ain't take mine." He unlocked his door, sat down on his empty floor, and fell asleep facedown in the dust.

The pianist's eyes were baggy. They looked like folds of dark red cloth, but it was an ugly dark red. He had been sleeping alone on his bare apartment floor for two weeks now. His hands still ached, but now his back ached, and his neck and legs. His feet ached, too, from walking. He could no longer afford cabs. He could no longer afford anything, really. He was sitting at the bar now, drinking bourbon, though he couldn't afford it, either. He sat and sipped, and tried not to think about too much of any-

77

thing. He knew this was not how things were supposed to be. He was supposed to have a carpet on his floor, and a bed, and a piano. His hands were supposed to dance across the piano keys. This bourbon was supposed to be warm to his lips and even warmer in his throat and stomach.

The bass player approached the bar. He was the designated pariah. The drummer and guitar player had told him he had to do it, though he didn't want to. His father had played with the pianist. It would be like losing a member of his family. But he looked at the pianist, sitting there, eroded, and he thought of it like he had thought of euthanizing his old dog, thought "It'll all be for the best."

"Hey, man," the bass player said as he sat down next to the pianist. "You doin' okay?"

The pianist looked up. He forced a wide smile, like shucking a piece of worm-eaten corn. "Little B!" he almost shouted. "Glad you made it over here to the bar for once. Let me buy you a drink. What you have? This dude," he said loudly to the girl next to him, another cute know-nothing, "is the best up-and-coming bass player in the city. Has he got some hands!" The girl smiled shyly, looked at the bass player, who was probably only ten years older than she, then turned back to the man on her other side.

The bartender brought the bass player a drink. He paid for it himself. "Put that money away, man," he said to the pianist. "You ain't got enough to be tossin' around like that."

The pianist flashed a thick green wad at him. "What you talkin' about? I got mad money, man, mad money."

"All ones," the bass player noticed. "You probably got your-self about twenty dollars there."

The pianist ignored him. "I been thinkin'," he said quickly, "'bout our playin' together. I guess you guys been thinkin' 'bout that, too."

The bass player nodded slowly. "Kinda," he said. There was a television set next to them. It was too loud. The bass player turned it down a notch. "Yeah, we been thinkin' 'bout that some. You first."

"Well," the pianist said. "Well. Well." His gaze was set on the girl next to him, the one who had turned her back to him when he started talking. She was kissing the man next to her. They had probably just met. "Well, I been gettin' to where I need the music more, man. You know? Like some dude said, I don't know who, maybe Ahmad or Miles or somebody. Jazz is a med-icine, you know? It soothes the soul. Guess I'm just now real-izin' that. You thought about that much, man?"

"Some," the bass player lied. He was watching the girl, too. He bet he could get one like that. He wasn't so old, really. Only about thirty. But he looked old sitting here, next to the pianist.

"So I been wonderin'," the pianist said, "whether you dudes want to play some more durin' the week. More than three days, say? Maybe more like four or five. Six, even. I miss the music, man, when I'm not around it."

The bass player said, "Oh." It sounded like a hammer hitting a stringless damper. "Oh," he said. "Well, uh. Well. We hadn't really talked about that."

"What you talked about?" the pianist asked. He was looking

at the bass player now. He was looking dead at him. The bass player looked away. He shifted uncomfortably.

"Hold on," he said. He walked back over to the drummer and the guitarist. They stood together and talked for a while. Then they all walked over to the bar.

"Hey, man," the guitarist said. "I guess we got to tell you this straight up. Hate to say it, but we're lookin' for a new piano player."

The pianist sat very still. They thought for a minute he might not have heard. Then he said, softly, "Why?"

"Aw, c'mon, man, you know why," the guitarist said. "You lost it. It's gone. The fire, man. You don't have it no more."

"I got fire," the pianist murmured.

"Then where is it? We sound awful, man. You can't even make it through a solo no more. We can't do this now. We let you stay on for a long time, but somethin's gotta give."

They watched him sit there. Then he stood up violently, suddenly angry. "I don't have to take this!" he said. "I played with your fathers! I played with Miles, man. I played with Miles and Buddy DeFranco. You ever play with Miles? He told me I was the best. The best, man, the best he'd ever sat in with!"

The guitar player shook his head. "Miles is dead, man. De-Franco's been dead for twenty years. Your fingers's shot. I'm sorry to say it, man, but you just can't play no more."

Slam. The pianist put his glass down on the table like it was filled with mercury. Everyone in the bar was looking at him now. "I'm the best!" he screamed at the guitarist. "I'm the best in this damn city. Everyone knows that. If you can't handle playin' with the best, then you can lose it!" And he whirled around and walked out of the bar. The bass player ran after him. The guitarist shrugged. The drummer walked back to the stage.

Outside it was dark and alive. The bass player caught up to the pianist, who was walking briskly down the street. "Hey, man," he said. "I'm sorry. I'm really sorry."

The pianist ignored him. He took his sunglasses out of his pocket and put them on. He looked ridiculous. Most of the streetlights were out.

"It's dark out here," the bass player said. "You know it's dark, right? Lemme call you a cab."

"Believe I'll walk," the pianist said. "I got a date tonight in another bar. She's meetin' me there." And he strode away.

"I can lend you some money," the bass player called.

The pianist kept walking. He crossed the street. A truck passed, loud and obdurate, behind him. The bass player stood watching him for a long time, until he was out of sight.

One of the hookers leaning against the lamppost called to the bass player. "Hey," she said. "Isn't that old guy famous?"

The bass player nodded. It was getting faintly light above the buildings. "Yes," he said. "He's a very famous man. Very famous."

— Chris Gibson

Ska Show Saturday

I merge effortlessly onto I-35, like a plane coming in for its thousandth landing. My car weaves itself through gruelingly slow traffic as I pass by the glowing commercial signs of Ed Noble Parkway. My car takes the route it has taken many times before, with almost no thought from me. Anticipation rivets me as I approach Moore. My excitement can barely be contained as I contemplate how long I have waited for this day. My body vibrates with the rhythm of the road gliding beneath me and the bass produced by my own stereo, which is blaring at the loudest humanly tolerable level. As I pass through North Moore's own Tornado Alley I am overcome by panic. I reach down to find the volume knob. The music fades, my anticipation turns to dread, and loud music doesn't seem to be the best remedy. The highway that accepted me at the beginning of my trip is now attempting to trip me up. Each bump in the road is a hill, and each car, a giant invading my path. As I enter South OKC, I frantically wheel down the windows of my car. The wind running over my body is a cleansing shower for my distressed thoughts. When I reach Crossroads Mall, I escape the ghost haunting me, by way of the I-240 exit. I begin to feel at ease, as I am overcome by my experience as a musician. Performing fades away as a worry, and becomes merely an extension of my usual bodily habits. I-240 passes by in what seems like a matter of seconds. As I pull up to my venue for the evening, I know I am mentally prepared to play. I exit my car, trombone case in hand, preparing to lose myself for the next few hours.

The CD store is an epileptic seizure of posters and stickers.

I pause and wait for my eyes to adjust to the frenzy of color. Once they have, the image steadies. I arrive first. The room seems to quiet, and I feel that I should create some sound in this empty hall. I walk to my place and unlatch my case with a satisfying click. I am welcomed by the silver glare of my horn. I begin to piece together my horn, like a mechanic fine-tuning a car, although I go about it with much more care. When all the joints have been screwed together and the slide has been oiled, I inspect my trombone for imperfections. I run my hands over dents and scratches and frown at my own carelessness. However, it still plays as it did the day I got it. I step outside to warm up. My tone on the first note can be likened to that of a dying horse, but I know it will improve. By the end of my warm-up session, my trombone is turning air into a cloud of tone that fills the night sky around me. I head back inside where my bandmates are now setting up. War sets in. The drums lash out with sporadic rhythms like gunfire. The guitar and bass attempt to tune but only succeed in creating dissonance, like the engine of an overhead bomber. The microphone checks as well as the shouts of concertgoers drown in the clamor, like random commands on the battlefield of the band tuning up. The trumpet interrupts with the occasional call of reveille. My eyes train from bandmate to bandmate; everyone appears to be ready. Time to start.

The first note explodes from my bandmate's bell and bounces from all four corners of the room. The ears of the crowd perk up like the ears of a dog that hears its owner pull up in the driveway. Their heads swivel, mouths agape, as if they didn't expect a concert to break out in the middle of their conversation. The first seconds of the song consist of horn intros and a building guitar line. The audience's attention shifts toward us. Crack! The drums come to life and so does the crowd. Electricity seems to run throughout the throng of people, connecting their hearts to pulse at a uniform rate. It is this energy that feeds and dictates our actions. The smell of sweat and the metallic air from my horn take up residence in my mouth. A cumulonimbus of cigarette smoke forms near the ceiling. My eyes close to avoid the acidic cloud — I no longer need to see. The thump of the bass drum and snap of the snare, on two and four, create a rhythm that contains me, like walls I can't break through. The low, modulating hum of a walking bass line provides a floor on which musical thoughts may stand. The guitar rings above on the offbeats like a ceiling that holds me in musical check. This creates a room that restricts me, yet leaves me to explore modes and scales. Our sound personifies ska. I step up to the microphone for my solo. I spread my feet and brace myself for the frenzy of notes that I know will soon fly from my bell. My mind goes blank, and the sound bounces to every square picometer of the room before it comes back to me and gives me a chance to hear what I did. My trombone falls to my side, and the crowd shouts its appreciation. I smile with satisfaction. Our set slams and jumps itself to the big finish. The distorted guitar pummels the room like the clamor of two giant gears grinding against each other. I fill my lungs to their bronchiole-exploding maximum and let my last note scream until I collapse to the floor in a fit of contentment.

When I recover, I rise and walk outside. My sweat glands go hyperactive. I realize that it had been an inferno inside. During the show my mild euphoria had blinded me to the needs of my body. My leg muscles throb with the beat of my heart. My lips have turned to a warm jelly substance. My ears are ringing to the same rhythm that my legs throb, and none of this mattered until I stepped outside. Another band begins to play inside, but I can't find the energy to go watch. I grab the bottle of water next to me and pull it across my forehead. The lukewarm water feels like ice to my burning body. I open the cap and absorb the contents like a dry sponge. My tongue, now more than a brick sitting in my mouth, can offer words of thanks to my congratulatory friends. Slowly I recuperate and head back inside, where another band is starting its war of "tuning up."

The lights go out and the room is bathed in red light. The band steps up to their microphones, and the players begin to thrash against their instruments. I am now part of the crowd. Crack! When the drums come to life, I come to life. My arms and legs jut out in random spasms that can only be known as dancing. My mouth develops a warm sandpaper taste as I continue to shout along with the lyrics I have heard hundreds of times before. The overexerted crowd has sucked all the oxygen out of the room. The stale, acrid air fills my nose and mouth but doesn't provide anything for me to breathe. The only way to respirate is to jump up into the air with the rhythm of the music and catch some oxygen hanging near the ceiling. The band's horn players sprint out into the audience and join our dancing pulse. Their slides rocket out at blazing speed as they play the tune and narrowly miss the heads of a few innocent patrons. The trombone player moves to the front of the audience. He assumes the same stance I took earlier and wails on a pristine solo. His tone slams me in the face, then slowly trickles down my spine, pulling chills with it. Their set bumps and grinds its way to the big finish. Bodies start to bounce off one another like Ping-Pong balls in a lotto machine. All around me, everyone experiences the same muscle-throbbing, vocal cord–stretching, smoky-eyed, ear-wrenching, carpet-grinding, distorted air euphoria. Then the band stops.

The crowd races to the door. It funnels out like cattle in a stockyard, searching for a breath of fresh air. Now only the occasional click or crash of the band tearing down their setup disturbs the peace of the room. I stand in the middle of the floor. Finally, I resign myself to the fact that the euphoria will not last forever and limp outside to my car. The salutations and shows of appreciation from my bandmates and members of the other bands now sound distant and faded. I reach up to pull the cotton out of my ears but don't find any. I unlock my door and get inside. The level of my stereo, which used to be humanly intolerable, is now comfortable. My car heads itself for our usual postshow hangout, Taco Cabana. Once again, I arrive first. I wait under the haze of a streetlight. The streetlight is surrounded by a swarm of crickets and moths, to the point where it produces nothing but the occasional streak of white clarity to invade the darkness. The faint smell of grease wafts through the air around me. The earth shakes as bass blasters on wheels pass by, dropped low enough to bottom out on an ant. My friends pull up and we head inside. Every fluorescent combination imaginable accosts my eyes as we enter the restaurant. I shuffle up to the cashier, who is standing firm guard over her post like a bulldog. I offer my order of two fajita tacos and step aside. I stare over at the salsa bar. It looks like a garden that got lost, and found its way into a deco Formica kitchen. I sprawl out into my fluorescent black chair and dutifully nosh on my fajita taco. My bandmates and I attempt conversation but know it is well past curfew and we should be home. I stumble out to my car and fly off.

My body calls out for sleep, so I fly a little faster. It seems like days since I made this trip to the City. Then, I had concentrated on emotions, I couldn't wait to lose myself in the moment. Now, all that calls to me is my body. The underdeveloped muscles in my legs send sharp electric jolts to my nerve center. They had not worked like this in months. A fajita taco swells in my stomach, promising the onslaught of heartburn in the near future. The ringing in my ears is replaced by a pounding in my head. However, I still experience the hearing loss to prove I was there. The rattle of a bottle of Advil and the familiar comfort of my bed call me homeward. I lost myself to euphoria for a few hours tonight, and my body is going to make me regret it tomorrow.

— Grant Slater

Daydream

Molly Molly Molly Molly Molly Molly
      Ringwald.
That's who i am asking to prom
and i'm going to say Molly Ringwald,
will you be my date for prom because
your face is on my t.v. screen all night
and on my brain all day and
your pain is my pain and i am also
ecstatically fumbling from time to time
and i love you movie-sized, the kind of way
where everything hurts just a little,
where it's hard to touch the first time
but when you do you can't let go until
the camera pans out far enough to
make us dots together on the landscape,
so will you go to prom with me because
there is no one in this world who knows me like you do
and . . . and . . .

you'll let me down easy because you know
that is what i really want.

— Harris Feinsod

Painting to Berlioz

Ever since Richard left, I have been sleeping in one of the T-shirts he forgot to take with him — but I don't mean to be maudlin about his leaving. It's just that his shirts are worn and comfortable. No, I'd have to say I'm glad he's gone.

This is what I told Don when he asked why I never sleep in something sexy.

All he said was, "What's maudlin mean?"

I tucked my knees to my chest and pulled the worn green shirt over them. It was the same color as the walls of my favorite professor's classroom. That professor had said once, "Never share a house with an illiterate. Even for sex."

Richard never read much, either.

At least the name Richard sounds like it might belong to an educated man. And he was educated; he went to college. I hate Donald, which sounds like an old fart or a duck, and Donnie, because it sounds like a teenybopper. Don sounds like some brawny laborer, which is exactly what he is.

That's what we are. A buff guy and some girl with breasts. Still adjectives to each other despite the time we've lived together. Still words we'd put on a list of attractive characteristics when we were in high school — and that's what I used to want.

When Don woke up this morning, I thought about saying, "Get out," or "I want to talk," or any of the dozen other things you say when you wish someone didn't know what you look like naked. Instead, I pushed him out of bed and made him bring me coffee. He has a decent memory about these things: a drop of milk, no sugar.

The last night, I fell asleep without knowing where Don was, and I was still sleeping when his friend Martin dropped him off. He climbed onto the bed, woke me up by kissing the insides of my thighs, where my marks show beneath the hem of a T-shirt.

I tried to swat him away, and he said, "Lie down." When I came, my back arched — I thought I could fly away from him. On another day, I might've jumped out the window and tried, but Don stood up and tucked the comforter across my breasts, and I fell asleep while he was changing into pajamas, humming "I Believe I Can Fly" as if he were the soundtrack to my life.

When I got dressed in the morning, there was a thick stripe of sweat on my nightshirt where it had folded into the ridges at the bottoms of my breasts. That line was diagonal; it interrupted the pale stripes of the shirt at irregular intervals.

"How long have I been living here?" Don asked.

"Seventeen weeks." I always know dates. It seemed like forever, although Richard lived here for two years and it felt like nothing once he was gone. "No coffee today," I called. If I was already thinking about Richard, I wouldn't need coffee, the same way I always woke up before the alarm clock when I dreamed about him.

"You know," I said, stepping out of the bathroom, "we have to talk," although I wasn't sure what I wanted to say.

"I'll pack," Don said, before I had time to think. "Martin'll take me to his place."

I hadn't been planning to ask him to leave, and I wouldn't ask him to stay, either. He was humming again, "You Were

Meant for Me" this time. It made me want to hug him, it was so inappropriate.

It was boring not to have to fight because someone changed my Mozart to Berlioz or the Stones to the Beatles when I was trying to paint. "They're similar," Don always said. "Same time period. I just like this one better." I painted to Berlioz for days after Don left.

I couldn't believe it made me lonely to think about not fighting. Like I said, I don't get maudlin about Richard, and I loved him.

On the days when the house was emptiest, I used to be careless in the kitchen so I could pretend it was Don's mess I was cleaning as I prepared a second meal. The meals I cooked slowly became more complicated as I spent longer in the kitchen.

When I'd gotten to like the way flour touches sweaty feet, I stopped spilling things that I could name after Don. It wasn't penance, stopping; I didn't need another person in my house anymore.

Painting to Berlioz became a ritual. I stopped hearing colors in Mozart, and though I'd never heard color in Berlioz, there was enough frenzy for the motion within the canvas to take over.

It was easier to work in movement than in color. I've never been a realist; with each variable I left out, I could concentrate more on the parts of a painting that were important. I'd once thrown away a still life Richard brought home because it never looked any different at night than it had looked in the morning. He thought I was crazy when I told him good still lifes move as much as any other good painting.

He was naive, and we left it at that. He wasn't qualified to argue with me about art, and I wasn't going to let him off because I loved him.

After all, the only time I ever saw Richard draw was the day I invited him into the studio for a charcoal lesson and we ended up on the table with the wispy charcoal turning us black. He said we'd ruined his picture, but I told him, "Love smears" and included it in my next show.

Richard understood when I wouldn't sell it after several offers. "That's why paintings move," he guessed, "love."

We tried to do a series in the same manner. The other pieces looked too deliberate, and I told him why paintings change position before I figured it out myself. "Spontaneity," I said, during orgasm. I think he might've been jealous, at least until he realized it wasn't a name.

I didn't rebound until maybe six months after Don left, which I suppose would mean it wasn't technically rebounding. There was a day when everything was turning red and fiery and I thought I might have seen love. I saw two sixty-year-olds push each other into the shallow creek, kissing and laughing. I saw a little girl feed blackberries to her friend, who licked the juice from her fingers as if they were her own. In the mirror, I saw a woman realize she had nothing to cry over.

I absorbed this all with a pencil. It swooped over the page in half-moons, the antithesis of the lines people become when they are still and you are not.

That night, I wanted to drape myself over some man at a bar and kiss like teenagers. It wasn't about love this time; it was about the ideal of kissing someone and thinking you might be able to love him. It was about the kissing itself, how something sexlike could be as aloof as it was intimate, sometimes even more so.

It took me a week to work my way into a bar. I drank slowly that first night, so that, should a decent-looking man appear, I might be coherent. Of course, he never showed up. He left me to find my own way home drunk.

It worked that way every day for a week. After the alarm clock went off, I fell out of bed and made my coffee myself because there was nobody else to make it. Whichever of Richard's shirts I'd slept in would go into the hamper when I got dressed. I'd paint—to Berlioz, of course—for a good portion of the day, and at some point I'd cook. I usually ate well before I'd go off to drink. I knew I'd be driving home each of those days.

It became routine. One day, I was surprised: An attractive man actually conversed with me. He drawled, like most of the men I know.

His name was Richard. On a hunch, I asked what he thought of Berlioz. When he frowned, I thought the two Richards might, someday, blend in a spiral of daydreams of things I've lost.

He invited me for a walk in the wind. The beach was right

there, and we left our shoes and socks by our cars and walked barefoot in the sand, although it was November. After a few minutes, he grabbed my hand and we started skipping.

"I'm a textbook romantic," he said, eventually, and kissed the split ends of my hair, twisting in the wind.

When I got home, the wind was sucking the curtains flat against the screen. I dug out a basketball shirt (the kind with two layers of material with little holes) that Richard gave me and slid into bed, my breasts spilling out the armholes. I stretched the red cloth over one of my hands, and with the black showing through, it looked like a strawberry, flattened on canvas.

— Jena Barchas Lichtenstein

Questions

Everyone says they know what love will be

And I say have you ever been?

Everyone says you get goosebumps when you touch your soulmate

And I ask if maybe they were just cold

And when everyone says they feel faint around their other,

I just laugh and ask if they ate breakfast

And when they say it seems that they know you better
than you know yourself

I always asked how they couldn't know themselves well at all

And then when I met you

I stopped asking questions and started listening to my heart

And maybe they were right all along.

— Katherine Casula

The Battle

Helen, the half-goddess,
She has divided me across a wall.
My love sits on one side,
And my lust paces around the other.
When I touch her,
The battle begins,
And Troy is set to burn.

— Matt McDonald

The Red Divide

How could I love a girl so much? I'm only sixteen. In my infancy, how do I love? Is it arrogant to assume that a mere newborn could find love? I, recently having sprung from one vagina, search for another to crawl into: hers. But she is so much more complex than the physical attraction that was the impetus for our original bond. She is warm, her skin soft. Her chest and arms cradle my overgrown body. She is a girl, not even a woman; I am a boy. What is it to be a girl, a girl loved by a boy? Maybe the love I found, the treasure, is fool's gold. Nevertheless, fool's gold never seemed so real. My love for her is as real as it can be, but there is a fence between us: our gender. That which makes her so attractive to my hormonal lusts also keeps her perpetually at bay. The female is the antithesis of the male; the sex organs are opposites, and yet we combine to complement each other.

Today, she was a girl and crying. A Hispanic male, 5'7", medium build, had just waved his penis at her in Central Park as she scurried home from school. Her scurrying was promoted to a full-out sprint as humiliation sealed her lips. With her bookbag bouncing awkwardly against her thigh, she ran away, towards nothing. They say adolescence is the defining period of our lives. Wouldn't that be funny? The only humor here lingered on the breath of the drunken perpetrator. His friends had watched a girl squirm and run under the oppression of the male sex. When she arrived at her house, solace came in small doses. Her first impulse was immediately to call me, her child of a boyfriend. What is in that word, *boyfriend*? Society fills it with meaning as if it were an ice-cube tray. Her call sparked my deepest concern as she related every singeing detail of her ordeal. Despite the pain and sorrow I felt for her, I could not truly share her experience. Love was not enough; it fell short. Although my every word was drenched in sympathy, it was far from comforting to her, for I was a boy, a male, a tall Y-chromosome who had never had another man wave his penis at him. I had never had someone call me names as I walked down the street. A woman has never grabbed my ass or said that she wanted to fuck me where it counts. No, my manhood has exempted me. I've been left out because I have a dick. Fortunately, I have been spared these harmful experiences; unfortunately, these experiences were a little too foreign, a little too alien. All the sorrow I felt for my baby did not add up to one single drop of genuine consolation.

How could a boy, not even a man, begin to crack at the husk of that which is female? I remember one time she had her period. It was always comforting when it came, for it absolved me of responsibility: It was proof. How could something so natural be so bloody? The definition of a woman was to bleed profusely for a quarter of her life.

Her blood seeped out of her as a constant reminder of her sex. To me, sexuality had not been part of my life much at all. It was the fleeting sensation of lust, a subtle itching, or a less subtle twinge. Sexuality for her was a weapon used to hurt. It had scarred her, leaving an everlasting wound, the scab of which refuses to heal. Every day of her life, men and boys had, do, and will bombard her with constant reminders of her place in the patriarchy. Sexuality is a weapon, a tool, our vessel for domination. The girl who fights back and uses her sex is dirty, a whore. Single-sex pedagogy, by the exclusion of girls, had taught me that they hinder our progress, that their sexuality is a fleeting and insignificant distraction. Save the homoerotic undercurrents, there is no sexual expression at an all-boys school. That void in my life had defined hers. Girls, in school and life, come under a constant barrage of fire about their bodies and sexuality. Their breasts and thighs are served rotisserie style to men. Overuse of her sexuality is dirty, underuse is prudish. The male libido has cut women, her, and their remains a scar that bleeds.

My penis defined natural for me. This definition was erected to place the male race in the center, with all others on the outskirts. I had built a cage around myself without even acknowledging its presence. I could not see, I could not feel, I couldn't even touch a woman, a girl. She described her period as a "slight trickle" of blood; the flow would find her inner thigh, alerting her of its presence. What was it like? What if blood came out of my penis once a month, or dripped out of my ears, or was secreted through my scrotum? What if this was a part of me? Maybe it was like a cut down there. A cut, however, implies a deviation from the norm, an injury — her period was a part of her; it was her definition of natural.

I was the one waving my penis at her. I love that bloody girl.

— Nicholas Zaniska

Virgin

The Virgin Field is a place where clear-minded boys ride rusty red bicycles and attempt to hit the towering telephone wires with pebbles and paper airplanes. The only way to get there is to follow one of two roads, a north road or a west road, both of which are beds of chalky white shells. The north road bends through layers of thick pine trees, and the west road lays a straight path parallel to a railroad track that hasn't held a train as long as I can remember.

Everything there is natural (except for the wires), and there seems to be a perpetual gray fog that makes the sky hazy and dull whether it is sunrise or sunset or in between. There is a lake that appears to be endlessly long and lethally deep, though there are only a few inches of water above the smooth, stony bottom. In the middle of the water, there is a tree that has no leaves regardless of the season, a tree as gray as the fog. Everyone in the town considers the field to be one of the most beautiful places for miles around. I find it funny, though, that the only people who ever visit are the bike-riding children and myself. My name is Harmony, and I am sixteen.

I visit the Virgin Field constantly, and I drive there in my bright red car on the north road. When I reach the black forests surrounding the lake, I park behind trees so the metal doesn't pollute my view. Then, I sit and paint.

Three weeks ago, I took my paper and watercolor set, sat on the edge of the lake, and painted the naked tree. I dipped my brush in the clear brown water in front of me, added a tint of black, and streaked the gray thing, trunk, arms, and fingers. I splattered leftover black paint around the base and made the result appropriately misty, and I felt free to add fiery undertones of blue and orange even though they were only real in my imagination. I saw so much color in that drab place. A boy and a girl, no more than six, rode past, and their rusty handlebars were to me the color of cherries.

I blew gently across the moist sheet and placed it in the passenger seat of my car. Driving back down the curved north road, I kept my eyes focused out of the side window and watched the tree until I couldn't see it anymore. I heard the dusty shells breaking below the wheels.

Eventually the road comes to a four-way stop that never has any traffic. I come to the stoplight. It shines a vibrant red. I sit and wait, not thinking. No other cars cross my path, and when it changes color, I go home.

Every night I wait for the chime of my telephone.

"Hey."

"Hello, my love," I say. It is Robb, and I dribble my body like frosting over the arm of a wonderful pink chair, sinking in softness.

"My love?" he questions.

"I am pretending." Robb and I have an agreement that our friendship is only a friendship, and I play games with that notion. For the past two weeks, I have felt like a sixteen-year-old dancing around a midlife crisis. I am trying to regain something lost, I think. Perhaps excitement, or some new realization. I want to be like the seven-year-old I was, who had just begun to notice the enchantment that a boy could make me feel. I want to take Robb's hand and dress him up like a groom. I want to take him to the Virgin Field and arrange a pretend marriage. I want to be . . .

"Whatever. Maybe you'll find someone in college to play dress-up with you."

"I can't wait that long." Yes I can.

Robb never has a reason to call me anymore. He used to call me to go out, or to help him with his homework. Once, he needed my help in English. "It isn't hard," I said. "How much have you done?"

"Not much."

"How much is not much?"

"Nothing."

"You know, if I could meet a man who would stare straight into my eyes and open his red lips and whisper poetry to me, I would completely give myself to him." I didn't believe what I said.

"This stuff makes no sense to me."

Tensing on the chair, I sat upright and opened my textbook.

I live with my aunt, an old maid of about thirty-two, a secretary who spends her work hours reading three-dollar romance novels with titles like *The Texan Romeo*. She and I do not have a healthy relationship. While I drive to a field and push myself to rediscover my ability to do cartwheels, she sits in a stagnant, warm bathtub, which is where she goes directly after work, and where she dwells till bedtime.

At dinner three weeks ago, after I had painted the tree, she pointed out that trees are not blue, and that water is not orange, but otherwise, that it was a good piece. I thanked her and nibbled on the reddish meat she'd cooked for dinner.

Two weeks ago, I drove to the field and found I'd forgotten my paint. So I took a few sheets of paper I had and folded them meticulously into miniature airplanes. I threw them up to the telephone wires, and the fog pressed them back to the ground. I picked them up and threw them again and again, and it didn't bother me that they couldn't fly. I, like the boys on bikes, blamed it on the weather and not my poor paper-folding skills.

I walked to the lake with my jeans rolled unevenly to the middle of my legs and stepped, splashing wildly, into the water. It was cold and full of tiny, rushing currents that tickled my ankles like fish. And there was a fish. For the first time, I saw something in those few inches of water, an orange fish with carmine splotches that looked like rosebuds. I ran out, jumped into my car, and left for paint. I came to the intersection, and the stoplight blushed a voluptuous red. I sat and waited, and my heart pounded.

In my room, I gathered a bagful of colors, half of which I would never use, but would always try to. Pastels, watercolors, pencils.

Ring. I picked up the phone.

"Hello," I said.

"Hey."

I shouted his name.

"Yeah. . . . It's me."

"Robb, come with me to the Virgin Field, please. Please."

"What's there?"

"A beautiful fish."

"Why do I have to go see a fish?"

"You don't, but as my best friend, I'd like you to. Please. I love you, Robb."

"Fine."

He took the straight west road, and once there, I made him move his car behind the trees. I took my paper and stood in the center of the lake, stepping lightly, gliding my toes slowly through the water. He rolled his jeans and shook waves in the surface.

"Stop that. You'll scare him."

I couldn't find the fish. I turned, now making my own waves, frantically disappointed. I had lost it.

"Where is this thing?" he called, and I turned to see him standing on a high limb of the tree without a leaf of clothing. His skin was white with coldness. His jeans were laid carefully next to him, and he was ready to jump.

"Don't!" I shouted, and he managed to keep his balance. "Wait. Just stand there."

Without thinking, I sat down in the middle of the lake and propped my paper against my knees, penciling his straight body as wild water seeped into the fibers of my clothes. Where lake droplets had spattered against my skin, I felt frozen wind biting. Robb complained about that.

"Just wait," I said. "You can't jump anyway. It's not deep at all. It only looks deep."

His chest was vermillion on the paper, his eyes were ruby, as was the water. Ruby, not sapphire, like those eyes. The gray fog, more silver than gray, moved toward and away from his body in rhythm, blurring and clearing my vision, and I dug more colors from my soaked pockets. Stark against the sanguine figure was a magnificent green tree. I speckled it with the warm color of his skin and filled his young figure with rich, verdant shadows.

"I'm shaking," he whined.

"One minute. Just one more minute."

"I want to see what you have. Show me."

"One minute. Wait."

I gave it one last glance. I checked it ferociously for any needs. I breathed. I signed the bottom like a marriage certificate. I held it away and closed my eyes. "Here it is."

He climbed down from the tree and took it in his hands, stared for a minute, and dropped my work into the water, as we fell back together, locked. "So it is not with me as with that Muse, Stirr'd by a painted beauty to his verse," he began, his words like the wind. I felt a shell break away from my body, a released sea creature wading in a gentle whirlpool.

I drove along the north road and came to the intersection. The stoplight beamed a violent red, and I sat and sucked air into my throat.

We agreed to be friends that week. It was my request. I think that a moment of pure livelihood raped my innocence. I loved to look at things with a jeweled eye of fantasy, and on that day my vision exploded like a steaming volcano and emptied into the hard lake. I would fight to have kept it inside. I have a mind that now exists to be a child again, and I am convinced that I am not one.

The phone rings every night.

"Hey," Robb says.

"Love of my life," I reply. I think that he doesn't want love, and I think that I don't, either. I just want to ask for it, to pretend, like a seven-year-old, that it means something.

I am crushed apart.

A week ago, I sat at dinner with my aunt and noticed her latest romance novel tossed to the side of the table. I picked it up and read the title, *Eyes of Desire*.

"Do these books make you feel young?" I asked. The expression on her face was like a slap across mine. "I sometimes go to the field to feel young."

"You *are* young," she informed me. But she was lying. "Eat your meat."

That week, I pulled an old bicycle out of our shabby garage and rode along the north road to the Virgin Field. The wind crashed into my face. When I got there, I rode all around. I traced circles around the perimeter and wheeled the letters of my name into the grass. Harmony. My tree was still there. For some reason, this was significant to me. I didn't look for a fish. My feet were tired. I hated being on that bike, and so I turned around.

I reached the intersection, and the stoplight pulsed with blood-red. I did not stop. I sailed with the wind against my cheeks, and I heard the horn of a bright red car. It looked like mine, and its driver, luckily, pressed the brakes just in time. I fell, though, and scraped half of my body. Half of my body stung as if it had been attacked with needles. The driver, panting in shock, stepped out of the car, and a three-dollar romance novel fell from her fingers. She was on her way to my field.

For three days, I lay attached to a metal hospital bed, mechanical, covered with dingy white sheets. My eyes blinked open and closed for hours. I am still exhausted from it all.

I visit the Virgin Field and try to regain my ability to do cartwheels. It hurts. In a few weeks, I imagine that I might go so far as to reopen my Pandora's Box, that tempting paint set.

At night, I eat in silence with my aunt, and when she goes to bathe, I go to my room and wait for phone calls. They always come, and they are stuck in repetition.

I have found that illusion and innocence go hand in hand. In gaining the physicality of my thoughts, I absorbed a world that I have not yet become comfortable with. I work to rediscover confusion, the sensation of a strange depth in shallow water, an engulfing stream of color in apparent blackness.

— Mark Thiedeman

Postlude

Go now
In Sunday clothes
And contemplate the rain
Slapping such black earth: This Glory
Be God.

— Molly Patterson

A Close Encounter

The dragons came in through the open door
     and left by the window.
We didn't see them,
     but we found traces —
a few scales, transparent as onion-skin,
     remained on the window sill,
and behind the house I found places where
     they had pressed the soft grass beneath them
and stretched out their great wings and slept.

— Chris Gibson

Picasso's Painting

There is a total of three things
I wish to discover here. My life
is only so long. I want to know
how much can be said with the
white page and the thin line of
my pen. I want to know how
I look, drawing with my eyes
closed. Finally, I seek to learn
what motions it takes to make
a dove spring from the eye of
a woman, what measure of love.

— Rebecca Givens

Citrus

I.

When I turn off the lights, the bubbles in my bath multiply like bacteria in the darkness. They climb onto my submerged body eagerly, like sequins clinging to a sweaty tan, sparkling flashes in the blackness. They smell like citrus, like a Florida orchard, and I try to breathe them into me, but they form clouds around my cheeks, refusing to surrender. I think, maybe if I can get them inside of me, it will be Florida in my lungs, slender green vines blossoming tiny grapefruits in my capillaries. I imagine what it would be like to pull out my bath drain and fold myself into the pipe beneath it. It would be perfect, a thin cylindrical volume of me. Ready to greet the rust. Ready to travel the pipelines all the way to Florida.

II.

I once knew a girl who would eat lemons whole and plain, rind and all. Her teeth wouldn't even flinch. I tried it once, but my tongue coiled back like a serpent and I had to blink to keep my eyes from shedding the small, hard tears that were inside of them. She finished my lemon for me. She was a good friend.

She always wanted to go to Miami, to see the lady who posed on the front of our Miami Lemonade bottles. That lady was beautiful, with luscious black hair and straight white teeth and shoulders that were caramel cascades. She had a lemon in each hand, full bulbs of sunlight between her fingers. The two of us used to be amazed by the front of our lemonade bottles, but then one day the store stopped selling them. And the woman with the caramel shoulders faded away until she wasn't even a memory anymore.

III.

The day I tried to eat the lemon was when it happened. They tell me it wasn't my fault, but I was there, so I should know.

We were sitting in the back of her car, the lemon-girl and her brother and I. She was so close to me that I could smell her sweetly clean detergent. Her breath was a dry mystery of fruit on the side of my cheek.

We ate Tic-Tacs back then. We thought they were so cool, but we were particular about them. *Only the orange.* It was like a motto for us. *Only the orange.* I used to call her Tic, and she called me Tac. Tic and Tac. Two words, two puzzle pieces fitting together, two dusty hands linking fingers on the playground.

That's what I said again and again the night after it happened. "Tic, where are you? Oh God, Tic, Tic, Tic." Tick, Tick, Tick. The rhythm of the clock matched the beating of my own heart and the smooth drumbeat of my words.

IV.

Sarah McLachlan sings in the stillness of my room. Hers is the voice of the woman on our Miami Lemonade bottles. I'm lying in bed, still warm in the grip of my bath, still treasuring the whisper of bubbles against my skin. I wonder what it would be like to be a corpse — to see only darkness with eyes deprived of sight. Where does your blood go when you die? Does it lie still and cold in the spiderweb of dammed rivers that your veins have become, turning purple and frosty as winter envelops the underground?

"Tic," I say softly, "I don't know how to let you go. I don't. I never have." Tic tic tic. Tick, tick, tick. Time passes, never erasing what I did to the lemon-girl's life. Sleep comes heavy but easy — a soft belly of dark pushing down on me, a mouth with Tic-Tac breath singing dream songs in my ears.

V.

They said her brother was brilliant, but I knew him for his shiny braces, silver sun-catchers when he smiled. They were twins, the girl with lemons in her mouth and the boy with silver in his. His jaw was set that day, his lips closing around a dark crevice of metallic, star-filled black. He was playing games on his calculator, hands humming with pleasure, fingers aching as they jabbed at the numbered keys on his lap. 9 — jump. 7 — fire. 5 — run. His knees fidgeted under the looseness of the heavy seat belt that he had recently unfastened.

I popped a tiny orange bullet in Tic's mouth. "Only the orange," she called out as she caught it with her sour tongue. She unbuckled her seat belt to face me better.

We shook our hard plastic cases, watching them turn into blurs of orange as the Tic-Tacs inside of them jumped and sank back down again. We were babies with rattles and I had never realized that in every life there is a time for innocence to end.

VI.

It's morning now. The sunlight filters onto my bed like a layer of sugar sprinkles, a flutter of yellow gauze. All I can think about is Miami, about how I would do anything to go there, to see the lady with the thick black hair.

"Mom," I say, "I want to go to Miami."

"My Lord," she replies, "why would you want to go there?"

Good question, I think. "Well, We used to drink Miami Lemonade." Capital W, like We were divine. The holy duo — a pair of citrus breath-mints.

"That's not really a reason," she says, but her tone has softened. I have rights now, because of what happened to the lemon-girl.

I give up. The Miami Lemonade lady probably doesn't even live in Miami.

114

I'm not really looking for her anyway. I think I'm still looking for the lemon-girl, wherever she may be.

VII.

I'm guessing I lose a memory of her every day. Little memories, the kind that slip out the back door before you can stop them. I still have some, though, rich and textured like they happened only yesterday. Gritty clouds of sand dust crawling up our arms in the playground, bloody scrapes on our knees, scabs like thick sunrises. We were friends since birth; eleven years of feeling her palm sweaty in mine, of seeing the gaps in her teeth when she laughed. She had a cackle in her giggle, an edge to her smiles. She was always like that, a little more than you'd bargained for, one wisecrack away from getting sent out of the classroom.

The Halloween before she died we were pirates. There's a picture of us here, our tin swords drawn, our black velvet patches looking soft and gentle on our freckles. I pick up the frame and my fingers tremble. "Polly want a cracker?" I ask her tiny glossy face. Silence. That's how things are these days — I ask her questions and she doesn't reply.

VIII.

I popped a second Tic-Tac into her mouth and everything seemed to go wrong all at once. While her eyes glistened broad and white, the tiny pebble of orange lodged itself deep into her lemony throat, and she started to gag. It wouldn't have been too bad, I tell myself, if it had ended there. Her mother, one of those emaciated, anxious women who send their kids to summer camp with parkas, reacted quickly and instinctually. She tried to pull over without looking or signaling. We'd been in the left lane, and a van lumbering to our right hit us as we pulled into its path. At that moment my world descended into breaking glass and squealing breaks and one piercing, static scream. One scream that still echoes inside of me as the clock goes tic, tic, tic.

IX.

After the accident, I knelt over her brother's calculator. It had flown out of his window and landed intact on the pavement. I pressed the number five again and again. 5 — run. 5 — run. "Run," I told the boy on the screen. "Run, run," I told the boy with the sun-catcher braces, but I knew that he would never run again.

X.

I am on a bus now, rolling high above sweltering streets and tapping the glass with my tender fingernails. LA buses might run in hectic criss-crosses over the city, but they jiggle smoothly, like boats, as they do it. I am a pirate, on board my vessel as I sail across an ocean of urban grit. I put my creased palm over my eye like it's a patch of black velvet. Now everything looks far-away and close, at the same time.

The woman in front of me pulls out a slice of Florida key lime pie. It smells sharp but good — like fruit and tangled palm trees and whipped cream. She eats it meticulously, never losing a bite, the way key lime pie deserves to be eaten. The way I would eat it.

I decide to follow the woman when she gets off the bus. Basically, I have nothing else I want to do and as long as she's in my sight I can remember the tropical smell of her slice of pie.

The lady pulls the call cord and the sign at the front of the bus lights up — cherry devilish letters to my bleary eyes. She crumples a scrap of stationery and tosses it into the aisle. I bend to pick it up, slowly so that she won't see me. Unfurling it hesitantly, like it would crumple between my blushing fingers, I stare in awe. I can hardly believe what I see on the heading — MIAMI LEMONADE INC. Tic would be loving this, is all I can think. It looms there — a promise, an insult, a prophecy: Miami Lemonade. I feel nauseated for a moment, everything is so filled with the memory of her.

XI.

My mother once took us to a local fair, shepherding us through the fun like a pair of wayward sheep. I remember the way my damp pink cotton candy lurched inside of me when we rode the circular carnival rides. That's what we shared — seeing the world as an upside-down blur with our twin sets of tight eyes. Turned on our heads, the fair became a diffused checkerboard of twinkling lights and multicolored flickers of mist. Below us, booth keepers smiled as they collected dollar bills from children's eager outstretched hands. Kids paid to dream while we hung upside down and flew through the crystal air. We were happy in the cloud-misty darkness of the moment. We had no need for dreams back then.

In the chaos of those carnival crowds, there was one man who moved with smoothness and slowness and grace. As men in candy cane–striped suits thrust caramel popcorn and tiny trinkets into my anxious, quick-flying hands, I caught sight of an oasis in the confusion. He was a juggler of tangerines, a shaggy-haired man in a plum-colored wool vest who would bite through the fruits, skin and all, as they flew through the air. He winked at us as orange flashes obscured his grizzled grin. We giggled softly and watched the way his hands and mouth worked together like a well-oiled machine. His luminous white skin glowed in soft, curving comet tails against the darkness; our eyes were hypnotized by the gentle swaying of his fingertips.

All we needed then was to share that moment of smooth motion with the tangerine juggler and with each other. Little did the lemon-girl know that later I would keep her immortalized in that moment of magic.

XII.

I follow the key lime pie woman off of the bus and onto the sidewalk. We are in an industrial part of town, a place I have never been before. Warehouses loom up in silence on either side of me; the woman's black boots make muted clicks as they tap the asphalt. She wears a gray blouse and a black skirt; her hair is pulled back into a tight, painful bun. I realize I have never seen her face. To me, she is just a slice of Florida smells, a hollow seashell that resonates with sounds of the ocean.

She pauses at a large brick building and I'm not surprised to read the lettering on its walls. I feel that same lifting tug of exaltation as I gaze at MIAMI LEMONADE BOTTLING AND SHIPPING. The black letters, standing out against dusty red, begin to reopen all the feelings that have been half asleep since she died. I want her here so we can be the Holy Duo for this — this exploration of the factory. I lay my hand on the brick and it feels cool, like the glistening stacks of bubbles in my bathtub.

The lady keeps on walking towards the entrance. I realize that if I want to get inside I have to say something to her, a few words to explain why Miami Lemonade is so important to my pain.

XIII.

"What right do you have?" Her question echoed quiet and mean in the afternoon air. Her pasty arms quivered in the heavy light of dusk, her eyes were savage masks of gold-speckled hazel. "What right do you have to come here? To mourn what *you* did?"

I felt myself gagging inside. My own guilt was a toy in her wiry hands, unleashing her pain and deepening mine. I turned away from her then — the mother of my own best friend.

My dress was satiny black with tulle overlay. When I peered deep into its folds they became dark caves of hollow, shriveled sunlight. My fingers explored the fabric, searching for a home in the wasteland of black sheen that fit my body so perfectly.

I could feel the eyes of the lemon-girl's mother upon me. My shiny dress reflected her sorrow back against the tigress sun. One flick of my wrist, one orange flash from my Tic-Tac case, and here she was — staring at the double casket that was everything she had ever loved. I wanted to clasp her frail body in my arms — to tell her that at least her daughter had been loved, had been a best friend, had completed me like no one else could have. That made all the pain worthwhile, I wanted to tell her, that a girl could do so many wonderful things for someone else. But none of that seemed to matter anymore — to anyone but me. I didn't belong, even though we had been pirates together, even though we had seen the world as a twinkling blur of upside-down life.

XIV.

"Excuse me," I say to the back of the woman in the gray blouse. I look down, not sure what my plan is or what I will ask her.

"Yes," she replies, and her breath is key lime pie on my forehead. I look up and for the second time today I am amazed. She is the woman on the Miami Lemonade bottle. Her neck is caramel melted over taut vocal cords; her teeth are straight and white. I don't know what to say.

Suddenly, I have no questions; I just want to follow this lady wherever she goes — to be near the warmth and beauty that are in her. My eyes cloud up and I start to cry. My tears are sunny crucifixes of ocean as they run down my freckled cheeks. They are sparkling pearls — made smooth by the harshness of my longing to be near the lemon-girl.

"Don't worry, sweetie, we'll get you all fixed up," the woman says. She reaches up a French-manicured finger to brush away my tears. Her touch is feathery — a memory of Cocoa Butter against my skin. She

119

puts her arm around my waist and we begin to walk in silence. It is the un-spoken agreement between us that words would be out of place in our encounter.

XV.

The morning she apologized I was eating grapefruit. Wedges and slivers of sour juice, encased in membranes of translucent fruit-skin, slid between my teeth like fragile gems. They were all I could depend on, their consistency of taste and texture.

She covered her apology in beautiful sugar words; she plucked it out of herself and pressed it upon me like a forced embrace. In the end, it made me feel sour and used, like she'd had a mission to accomplish. Job done. When she rang I opened the door and we stood there, silent and uncertain. We were separated by the vast world that had been the lemon-girl's death; it hung between us, heavy in the morning. Finally, she spoke, as mothers al-ways do. "Come outside with me," she entreated, tugging at the curl of hair that hung like honey sunlight across her eyes. I could feel the grass between my toes — spears of dewy lime-colored jellyfish reaching towards the thick coolness of my heel.

"I can only say I'm sorry," she began, facing me resolutely. "She was your best friend, you were hers. You meant so much to each other and I for-got that so easily. You must know it was not your fault, it was no one's. It was destiny, in some form." She fingered the metallic cross around her neck. I looked closely at it; Jesus' face looked like a golden lemon in the flurry of day. I nodded but I didn't believe what she had said. "I'm sorry, I didn't mean for any of this to happen," I mumbled, shielding my words from her hazel gaze.

"No," she tried again, "you can't think like that. . . ."

But I was already off, running along the pavement towards a horizon that

I couldn't even see. 5 — run. I was the girl on the calculator screen. 5 — run. I was a digital escape artist without a home to call my own.

XVI.

I never would have guessed, but inside the Miami Lemonade Bottling and Shipping building is an atrium. It looms like a forest, like a Garden of Eden before me. But then I look up and see skylights instead of clouds, glass instead of wind. The woman guides me along a path lined with Japanese rice-paper lamps. The air smells like citrus and I think that maybe some kind of magic transporter has taken me to Florida. All around me, I see shimmering green; textures rise out of the monochrome like Braille poems. Peeking out of the plants are fragile fruits — kumquats, limes, oranges. They are beacons of light in a countryside of deep green mist. I want to leap off of the path and hide myself in the undergrowth so that no one will ever see me again.

The woman holds tight to my waist as we tread through this humid jungle. I look up when we stop and see that we have reached a clearing. A stone fountain gurgles before us, water clinging to its rough sides. Tiny icicle lights dangle through the vines above us like luminescent snakes, making me think of Christmastime in the city.

The woman begins to orient me. "Bottling is to our left, shipping to our right. All of the offices are up there, overlooking us." She sits down on a teak lacquered bench, smoothing out her skirt gracefully. "Now then," she continues, her armchair tour over, "you have something to tell me."

XVII.

We are best friends, I mean, before she died. She had a grin that was like sunlight sparkling on a chlorinated pool. My smile always felt like a reflex next to her glossy Mermaid lips.

The first time we drank Miami Lemonade was the summer we were ten. The vendor on the beach bike path, the one with gold teeth and a sinister cleft in his chin, sold us our first two bottles. They were frosty, dripping with crushed ice and filled with sherbet-yellow nectar. You were on them, but your hair was loose and flowing then.

I remember that night so well, the only night she ever escaped me. We snuck out of our families' summerhouse because the moonlight on the waves was too beautiful to resist. It was like silver slices of lunar soil were dancing on the froth of the tides — melting their flow into the deep blue ink-iness of the water. We rushed in to greet the lapping sea together — in our matching green-and-orange-striped bathing suits. It was so cold when we were in all the way but all I did was grip her hand tighter, pressing tiny grains of salt between our palms. We dunked our heads under at the same time, letting our hair strands move like sea snakes in the aquatic rhythm of cur-rent that had become our private world. Resurfacing quickly and quietly, I gazed up at the bulbous moon, shrouded in thin strips of white cloud. Her head burst through the surface, born again in the water, and I swear I could see constellations reflected in her hazel eyes. She looked so pretty in that light — her hair in thin matted streaks across her forehead, her mouth a strawberry crystal goblet. I can still picture the thin hairs on her arm, glinting like soft spines in the starlight. I still can't understand why I did it, but before I knew it I was leaning in to kiss her. I'd never kissed anyone and everything seemed so perfect, she seemed so perfect. But she ducked away from me, under the moving waters of the ocean.

A year later, she died in a car accident and I think that night is my most alive memory of her — of us together. Sometimes I wish I hadn't spoiled it by doing what I did — by driving her away into the darkness.

XVIII.

Her gaze is soft but penetrating, filled with all the words that I have just spoken. "Don't regret it," she whispers smoothly, and then she leans in to kiss me. There, in the filtered light of the atrium, we share emotions that have been bottled up in me so long I can't even remember when I last felt them. I've been kissed before, by passionless adolescent boys whose lips quiver and whose eyes gleam in conquest. But this is different, slow and innocent. Everything I ever shared with the lemon girl is in this kiss, all the unfulfilled promises I made to her in our years together. I begin to cry when our lips touch, when her cheek brushes mine. The Miami Lemonade woman is truly kissing me, is closer to me than anyone alive, has become my savior for one delicate moment in time. My sobs are choked and achy and salty. They escape into the green and glide through the plant-arched corridors like lost souls, wrapping around kumquats, skimming along vines. After my tears have come and gone, after my sobs have declared themselves lonely nomads in the air, it is pure exaltation. I feel like I am lifting up, up towards the skylights of the Miami Lemonade building. I am a hollow Tic-Tac, an iridescent bubble, a tangerine that is juggled. I am so light I have forgotten that it is even possible to be weighted down. And all the while she is close to me — my greatest dream, my greatest regret, all confused in the wide open places inside of me. When the Miami Lemonade woman finally pulls away, I realize joyfully that I have found the lemon-girl at last.

— Leslie Jamison

The Gift

Sweet sixteen and never been seventeen
Was all I could say
on the oh-so-monumental occasion
of my birthday, shining
like a gem in the distance, but proving
on closer inspection to be glass.
No party or car or fluffy pink dress,
No innocence.
My mother didn't know what to get me
Until she remembered the one thing
she never gave me as a child —
I had everything I wanted except one
pink-and-purple box containing
an Easy-Bake oven and several packets
of little-girl cake mix —
Instant innocence.
Laughing at this irony, crying
because my mother loved me that much —
Sweet sixteen and never had
Easy-Bake brownies.

— Sarah Dryden

In My Mother's Garden

A little girl will do crazy things for a tomato plant. She will tell it stories about her adventures in the scrambling woods and the dusty whispering night. She will water it with the greatest care, tilting the green watering can slightly to let the thin stream of water dampen the soil. She will even sing to it in her small child's voice that breaks and cracks. She will sing that song about the blue whale and the sea made of candy. Tomato plants are not too critical. They are good listeners, patient and unmoved, rarely given to fits of passion.

I loved to stick my hands into the dirt to feel the crumbling sensation between my fingers. The earthy smell of my mother's garden infused my hair and face. In the flower beds, poppies shed sweet pollen and grasses streamed like waterfalls. In the vegetable section, the herbs grew, roaming and untamed. My mother taught me the names of the herbs and I felt the words in my mouth. *Thyme, Rosemary, Chive.* Mint was always dominant, stretching its limbs and clambering over other plants. Rosemary was more secretive, crouching in little corners. Thyme was so delicate and whispering you could almost blow it away. I reached for basil, towering and uncompromising, shooting its leaves upward. Afterwards the smell lingered on my hands for hours.

When I was a little girl, my mother handed me a shovel. A shovel is cool and curved like the arc of the moon. Clumps of dirt usually cling to the spade. Shovels are for digging holes. Doesn't every girl want to dig to China? Doesn't every girl deserve to bury her hands in the dirt? I always wanted a tomato plant. I dreamed of picking the sweet red balls off the branches and plopping them in my mouth. My mother handed me a shovel. I pushed the spade through the damp ground. The soil felt like sand in a sandbox. Worms appeared in the black bread of the soil. Worms feel like chocolate pudding when you hold them in your hand. My mother said patiently, *This is how you dig a hole. This is how you carefully place the plant in the soil. This is how you fill a hole.*

I watched the pale cheeks of tomatoes turn glowing and flushed. They looked waxed and shiny under the sun. The small cherry tomatoes felt smooth and bulging when I touched them with my finger. I reached to gently tear one away. I let go of the branch and it swung back. I could smell the tomato before I tasted it. The sweet plum smell lingered before the red globe opened inside my mouth.

I am still hungrily prodding tomatoes with my fingers, searching for the warm explosion in my mouth. I wake up and run outside in my pajamas to dig my hands into the soil. I know the neighbors will be watching me through the creases in their blinds. I know how silly I will look when I come in to breakfast with dirt on my knees. But I can't stop pushing away earth. I still want to dig to China. I want to feel the dirt in my fingernails. The ground smells faintly of rotten tomatoes, soiled and buried. I remember this. I was a little girl and my mother handed me a shovel.

— Katie Fowley

A Dead Woman's Hairpins

Oh, did I love Christmas! The snow was piled high against the door; all the animals bedded down under an equally large amount of hay. The air was so cold that our nostrils froze during morning chores. And at night, when the coyotes howled far out on Mount Bennington, we could see the stars so clearly that it seemed there was nowhere to hide in the heavens. We'd gather by the fire with Cokes in our hands and sing carols to the strokes of Dad's folk guitar. Strings of lights wove through handcrafted school ornaments as the kittens pounced on the ribbons of unwrapped presents. Our three stockings hung together, silhouetted by the same fire. The greatest treasure of Christmas was that one of them read *Mom* in green cross-stitch.

My father has raised me almost since birth. He taught me how to deliver calves and lambs as the seasons changed. He taught me to read the storm clouds as they rose off Mount Bennington. He showed me how to fish in the mountain streams and how to climb the apple trees in the fall. He taught me traditions and values and the price eggs should bring on Sundays. He never had a son.

We planted a little sapling sugar maple in the front yard and hoped someday to draw sap from it as it grew to the size of its brothers. When the first thaw came in mid-February we'd have sugar-on-snow parties, just the two of us. We'd bring in great milking buckets full of snow and pour them onto cookie sheets, coating the powder with a layer of steaming syrup. I'd lick my fingers one by one, savoring each sugary bite. I lost eleven teeth on those days, gnawing away like a little wolf cub on the hard candy. Father Wolf would yank yards of paper towel from the rack and stop the bleeding. Popsicles and ice cream would precede the tooth fairy. I'd waken to return to school triumphant.

We were as close as a New England father could ever come to his only daughter. He was coarse and kind, a great teddy bear of a man. With closely curling red hair and a height that nearly scraped door frames, he lived up to the name O'Connor. He had a laugh that could shake rafters and a full Irish voice that cried ballads as he worked. He ran his farm as his father had and his father before that. The O'Connors were embedded in the town's history. The bank and public library bore the name.

Dad was there for me and gave me all he could, but I couldn't stop myself from looking at the pictures on the wall. As in any good Irish household, there were too many pictures to count. We had photographs of cousins and grandcousins and stepcousins that I'd never heard of or seen. Some were my grandparents — black, white, and stiff. Those ghostlike images were almost as foreign as the one in the frame beside my father's bed.

When I was younger, I'd lie on that bed and wait for him to come in after evening chores. The picture waited with me. Sometimes I'd press its golden frame to my heart. I'd run my finger down the glass so many times that the features were blurred with my greasy prints. I wanted desperately to meet that picture, to see it every day of my life. Hug it, have it teach me to make Christmas cookies and to sew. Have it do all the things my father could never do. But I saw her only once a year. During Christmas.

She'd sweep in the day before Christmas Eve, in a shining

car that overwhelmed our old Ford pickup. It was sleek and meant for the freeways of Boston, not the back roads of Vermont. Out of the trunk she'd produce presents, like Mary Poppins in an overcoat. First, she'd unload her overnight bags, then packages with plastic bows, and always last, a little black case. She'd carry her violin in as a finale to her wonderful arrival, holding it the tightest. It was her life, her child when she was away from the family.

She smelled of travel, that everpresent starchiness of airplanes and hotels. Her perfume was rosin. Her hair gave off a heavy scent of flowers from a bottle, but to me she smelled like angels. If there was a god for everything in the world, for lakes and streams and volleyball, then she was the goddess of music. I saw its power rock her small body as she played passionately for me. In her dark eyes at night as she leaned over, I could see the sheet music in her pupils.

She came for only a week, but her smell and her high laughter faded much later. And the longing in my father's eyes never went away. She cooked us a beautiful dinner, turkey and stuffing and peas and pies. She poked her sharp little face over my shoulder as I cut cookies out of dough, adding suggestions here and there. She looked over my schoolwork from the previous year, awed and impressed by my "great achievements." She read me Dr. Seuss and Pearl S. Buck and sang me the Beatles and Bach.

But then she left again in her city car, the snow flying back to us. Her music took her places and left us behind. From Tokyo to London she traveled, content only with the first's seat and a sold-out balcony. She slept in hundreds of hotels with hundreds of friends and left us all out of it. That was her way, she had told Father years ago. Her music was the most important thing in the world and nothing could tear her away from it.

If my father was my teacher, she was my ideal. I joined the band in sixth grade to no avail. Likewise the chorus. I primped in front of mirrors for hours, attempting to gain one milli-inch of her beauty, of her slightly slanted almond eyes and her round face with its slightly sharp chin. My lips were never full enough and my lashes never the right length. I tried pulling my dark hair back but was disappointed at the shape of my ears. I looked like an elephant, so I let my hair down. It was the color of soot, not a raven feather, and was always a little too straight. My skin was dark, weatherworn and naturally tan; hers was as white and fair as porcelain. She was petite and delicate, but I was tall and gangly and awkward for my age. Maybe I could have been taught grace and manners and makeup. But my father was a farmer and he knew nothing of mascara and blush. I never wore tights as a girl because he couldn't help me put them on. This didn't bother me until I was older, when I could look back and reflect, growing cold with anger at my childhood.

But now all I want to remember is Christmas and the smell of apple pie wafting from the kitchen.

On those golden mornings I would drag my parents out of bed at the first gray light. Stumbling downstairs in sweatshirt and fleece, slippers and socks, my father would plug the lights in and start a fire, while my mother captured the magic on videotape. There were red, white, and green packages with colored plastic bows, each bearing one name of three on its gift tag. Wrapping flew from under the tree as we all tore open our presents. Both of my parents were as undignified as I when it came to unwrapping. One by one the gifts were drawn from their tissue-paper nests; Barbies were cut loose from their impossible plastic reins; tags were removed from shirt collars. Mother loved my crayon drawing; she'd take it with her, treasure it forever. Candy canes and hot cocoa were for breakfast; pancakes and bacon came later on in the day, maybe when the sun rose. The cows needed milking and there were fresh eggs, but that could wait. Batteries were needed, searched for, found. She sprayed her new perfume, he tried on his shirt, and the day waltzed on. I tired of playing, fell asleep on her lap, smelled that new perfume from the fancy catalog. Leftovers were for dinner; I got carried up stairs in Father's strong arms. Where I slowly drifted off to sleep in bed with new teddy to the lullaby of carols played on violin.

Christmases passed. I began to grow into my arms; my legs were no longer too long for my body. I smiled and laughed and gathered friends. But I lived in her shadow. My smile wasn't as perfect as hers; it was simple joy, while hers was poised, beautiful. The two of us changed together. She was surprised at my height, at my newfound elegance, and I was surprised at her unaging charm.

But Mother continued to be a once-a-year occurrence. As one looks forward to a special vacation or holiday, I looked forward to her arrival. The rest of those middle-school years, I stumbled to the bus stop, fresh out of bed, and stumbled back home in the evening, equally tired. I cooked breakfast and dinner, studied math and science and English. I milked the cows and climbed mountains. I blew out birthday candles year after year. I was fourteen. Almost a woman, but so desperately wanting to remain a child, awkward and charming and everything young.

I was content to draw. I could sit for hours in the deepest concentration as if I was pulled into the beautiful worlds I created. I dreamed of my pastels taking me somewhere. I drew dreams: beautiful women in medieval gowns, beautiful men with swords at their sides, beautiful landscapes of castles and clouds. Pastels were the shades of my life, blurred at the edges but brilliantly smooth. I was dreams and giggles and nothing serious. But at the same time I was dark, overshone by a mystery woman.

I loved her desperately, as one loves a place they will never go, as astronauts love the moon and Christians love heaven. I loved my mother. She was that wonderful and remarkably beautiful place that could tell you all you needed to know and teach you to mirror its grace. She was mystery, my father explained, from a different land and different time, his fairy-tale bride. It was only fate that could have brought them together: fate that a friend had fallen so ill he'd had to step in, cello and violin seated near enough for stares. Oh, and how ironic that her car had broken down and he'd had to walk her back to her apartment. It was even fate that Father had decided to go to the music conservatory, but he was young and wanted to see so much of the world. And Mother was the world.

So perhaps no one knew her, with her gentle oriental mannerisms that vanished as she swayed with free passion to the yearning notes of her violin. Beauty and mystery, and . . . Mother! How I wished, how I prayed she would return! Leaning far out my window at night, catching sight of that first star and wishing, just wishing for her to tell me all those secrets she hid behind mystery and once-a-year wonder. I squeezed my eyes tight to prove to that first star how much I cared. Mother, please return to me.

Then one Christmas, when I was fourteen, she didn't return. The high beams of her fancy car were late. The clock ticked on. My smile faded slowly, slipping off my anxious, pressed-to-the-window face. Father began to pace, checking the phone messages over and over. I drummed my fingers, unblinking, waiting for the lights to pierce the darkness. Then the phone rang, loud and piercing, in the house that was holding its breath. I heard my father pick it up, mumble something in his resonating voice, then his heavy footsteps on the stairs. He opened my door shyly, as if I might be changing or doing something I shouldn't. There was tension between us. He was heavy; I was light and young and wanted nothing to do with reality.

He stepped into my room, hands trembling at his side.

"Rachael, I have something very sad to tell you." He walked slowly toward me. Placing his hands on my shoulders he said, "Your mother's not going to be coming this year."

I was shocked. This was tradition! It couldn't fail me! "Why? What's wrong?"

"Your mother" — he looked up at me. There were tiny tears starting at the corner of his eyes — "was killed in a car accident on her way here. That was a New York State trooper. Her car was hit by a logger. It was icy and no one was driving well. She was . . . killed instantly, they said. No pain." One tear trickled down his cheek and hung off the end of his chin.

So that was the end of my beautiful mother. Cleanly and swiftly, she was wiped from my dreams amid the swirling snow and black ice. I gripped my father's hand and we cried together, alone in her once-upon-a-time house. I cried for the woman who had always been a surprise to me, as if a holiday itself had been killed. Silently, my father left the room, longing to be with his grief privately. I was content to cry, alone in my dark room. Her friends would clean out her various apartments; they had the right to whatever she kept hidden there. There were funeral arrangements to be made and last wishes to be fulfilled. There were tears to cry and aunts who needed comforting. There were phone calls and letters and explanations. There were stories to tell.

The day we buried her was brisk, even for winter. It was the kind of cold that froze you to the bone and sucked all moisture out of your body. The wind jumped up and blew between black skirts and through thick coats. The hilltop was barren; the trees that surrounded the cemetery scraped their dry limbs together. A bare and unforgivingly gray sky stared down at us, unblinking. The sun was hidden. The graveyard was encircled by a simple white picket fence. There were generations of O'Connors buried together, from the very first immigrant family to my beautiful, worldly mother. The ground was frozen solid but mother had been cremated. The petite ceramic jug that held her smoky ashes (its slender curves and gentle black brushstrokes reminded me of her) required a hole almost too large to be chipped from the frost. But it was, and she passed silently into winter.

The priest read words that I didn't believe, but didn't mind him saying. They made everyone but me feel better. I didn't care if she walked in valleys or that the Lord was with her. She wasn't with me. Funeral flowers rained down like the brittle icelike snow that was just beginning to blow. Roses covered her grave like they once did her feet at great concert halls. Slowly, one by one, the guests wandered away, holding hands, leaning on one another's shoulders for support. Like black ants they moved downhill, towards their cars and their familiar warmth. I left my father there. I knew she was still alive, somewhere; that wasn't her body they'd buried but that of some other woman.

I lived in a house of ghosts. It was not the house I remembered from my childhood, which had ended that Christmas Eve. It had aged, as all things but memories do. The paint was peeling; there was a rip in the screen door. The windows were dusty; the floors scratched and dirty. And haunted. Or at least haunted in my memories. If I tried hard enough, I could see my mother standing by the fireplace, violin in hand, rocking back and forth with the power of her music. There were ghosts because I wanted them to be there; living with illusions was better than living alone. I pushed away from my father. Mother had not stayed with him, why should I? I did not need his nagging and concern. I was a woman. I could handle myself, I vowed, taking her violin out of the case for the first time, gently tuning the strings. I practiced. Practicing is when you prepared for something that would change your life. I practiced for her life, for my recitals in Tokyo and London. Hours went by. My fingers bled. My eyes ached, and my music trembled. I could play like her; I could be her. If I tried hard enough. If I practiced and practiced until I got it right, I could be my mother.

135

My father was stunned, confused. But he had his own grief. I was fourteen. I was a woman. I was beyond him. He was comfortable with his sweet eight-year-old daughter but not this young woman who was growing to look so much like her mother. His life was steady and patterned. It moved with the land and the rains and the harvests. We had times of joy, laughing together over memories, and times of silence, but mainly he allowed me to do as I liked while he did the same.

It was hard, I admit. I wanted so desperately to ask my mother all the questions that I had never gotten a chance to. Where were you born? Where are Grammy and Grandpa? Where was school? Do you ever speak Japanese? Do you like anime? Do you drink tea and wear kimonos and hang out fish kites on Boys' Day? Do you think I'm beautiful? Do you love me? But I didn't have that kind of courage when she was alive. Now I would build it. I would become stronger and better and more graceful and beautiful. Until I stood in the same light as she did, onstage with violin in hand. I would outplay her and outlive her and my daughter would know who she was.

Spring faded to summer, blurred together by mud season. The sunlight was gold; it pierced through the dark windows of my house and sent all the flying dust particles aglimmer. I stood in this light and played and played and played. Dad stared, asked me to come to dinner, to climb Washington again, to see a movie; I refused. Friends called, boys, neighbors; no, I wouldn't come out to play, I wouldn't swim today. I was going to practice. It was my medication. It took away all the pain, that forcing of more pain upon myself. I was becoming a different, more perfected person. Something in me called out that I was my own person. I wanted to draw, my hands hurt, I wanted to laugh and dance and be with my friends. But I ignored it. I practiced my violin; I believed that in becoming my mother, I might somehow discover who I was, where I came from, and where I was going. The violin played on and I was empty.

I was my mother; I had to clean and tidy. One summer day I recalled that my father never touched the attic. I assumed it was filled with rafters and dust. But perhaps there were treasures. Timing my departure into the world of kept-away memories with my father's to the field, I dashed up the attic stairs. Summer light was gushing golden through the windows. Dust indeed was everywhere, floating in the air, upon the skis and boots and boxes. Where would Mother leave her things? I wondered, and just what was I looking for? Why wasn't I practicing, or drawing? I walked from wall to wall, peering into boxes and bags, opening drawers and sweeping off dust. Near the double windows I stopped. Two chests lay dreamily in the golden light of the windows, like pirate's treasure rippling under water.

I opened the nearest chest and my breath caught in my throat. I picked up the silk; it was cold to my touch. I stood up, pulling the beautiful white kimono all the way up with me. My mother's. I could smell her rosin. I touched the silk to my cheek, then carefully folded it over my arm and knelt down to examine the rest of the chest. A streaming obi of powdery pale pink embroidered with white, and a pair of thongs. All so real and cold on my skin. These were real. These were real princess's clothes. I began to cry, picturing her perfect face. My tears fell on the wedding kimono. I folded it and placed it aside, afraid of ruining the silk. Rocking back and forth on my knees,

I called my mother's name. The dress did not answer. When the sobs were little more than a trickle of tears, I gathered the strength to speak again. "Mom." I picked up the obi and brushed it against my drying cheek. "Why didn't you tell me? Do you know how much I would have loved it?" There was no answer.

I shut the white silk kimono back in the chest that had hidden it for so long. These were mine. These were things that no one but me could have. I opened the lid of the second chest. There were photos stuck into the lid's inner binding. I took them all out and held them to the sunlight. They were old and brittle, some black and white, others colored but faded with time. I couldn't possibly piece them all together. The story was incomplete without her voice as narrator. I lined them up on the windowsill: a pretty little girl in her sailor suit clutching a violin that was far too big for her; an old couple whose faces were more wrinkled than their fine robes; an older, more elegant Mom in a short skirt with a more appropriate-sized instrument; a beautiful mountain rising over cherry blossoms in full color; a teenage boy standing in front of an airplane with a headband wrapped tight, bearing the rising sun; my father, younger, beardless, more handsome in bell-bottoms, standing in front of the Boston Public Library. The photos didn't fit together. The puzzle was so big. A whole life couldn't be filled with snapshots of mixed generations and locations. I began to cry again, and felt like a fool for it. I was crying for so many things. Through my tears I placed the pictures back in their places, like pegs in their holes; the photos belonged nowhere else. I caressed each person's glossy face. They were all my family. Somehow.

I dug deeper into the chest, uncovering a newspaper in Japanese, *Shojo manga,* and a hair dryer. All the little things that we love so much but don't sum us up. "Mom," I whispered, picking up an Italian cookbook. "How could you hide all this from me?" I came upon an ebony box, polished to the point that it shone in the chest's dim light. Wiping away a stray tear, I unsnapped the delicate gold lock. Her jewelry. Her beautiful and foreign jewelry. Here were her delicate necklaces and petite pearl earrings. Her thick gold bracelets and simple beaded chokers. These were the bangles she wore as a child, as a girl, as a young woman. What she wore when she was my age, I thought. At the bottom of the box I found a bundle of simple bobby pins that didn't fit with the gold and polished gems. Pins that once kept back the layers of silken hair that I had once desired so much and had slowly grown into. They were things she wore to school, that walked where she walked, through the busy streets of Tokyo and along lanes of cherry blossoms to houses and near to people I would never know. They went with her to Symphony Hall; they moved with her body as she played Bach. These simple pins arranged her hair for dates with a younger George O'Connor. They were her everyday companions and they knew so much more of her than I knew.

I picked one up, simple and black. I put it in my hair. This was my mother. And this, I said, feeling my own arms and my large feet in their summer sandals, is me. These are my grandparents, perhaps, and my uncles and aunts, I thought, looking at the pictures. This was my mother's past, part of my own but not mine entirely. I felt the calluses on my fingers. How foolish, I thought. These were not meant for my hands! These were for Mother's! Then I remembered: You are Mother, you can be Mother. But I laughed. And it felt so good. I laughed hard and long, and best of all, it was my laugh. It was free and young and had a future, not a destiny. I had everything I wanted. I had the answers. These were the photos and the dresses and the jewelry that I had been searching for. Perhaps not her words, her spoken responses to my unsaid questions, but I knew. I knew as I clutched her wedding kimono to my chest that I was my own person and Mother had willed it that way. She was herself and I was me. Just me. Part of her, yes, but with my own past, and such a wonderful future.

I stood up, slowly and gingerly, reveling in the feeling of my own body's movement. Tenderly shutting the chest, I wove through the boxes and ski poles to the stairs. Leaving the musty smell of memories behind, I entered my own room. I returned the violin to its case, threw away the music, and picked up my pastels and drew. I drew myself as I saw myself: young and troubled, but beautiful. I needed no mirror. I drew her, as I remembered: short, but regal and overwhelming in presence. Her beautiful eyes and face and smile glorified my page. And they hung side by side, mother and daughter.

One day I'd add these drawings to my portfolio. One day my teachers would be awed by them and I'd win my future off them, but for now, they were proof of her music and my own talent. I would return as a teacher to that same old town that I grew up in with them in my pack. I would tack them up on my classroom wall. Each year a tentative student would ask who they were. I would answer, "That's my mom and this was me a long time ago." They would inspire those kids who knew nothing but pastures and chores to pick up a crayon and draw, to open up a small window to their own magic lands.

And one day I would wear my own wedding dress. Not the beautiful white kimono. On that day, I would wear my mother's hairpins in my dark hair. And I would know she was with me.

— Meghan Baxter

When You

When watching someone die, you must be very quiet. Always look down at the ground and examine your feet. Be uncomfortable and very somber. Allow your eyes to fill with tears. You will bite your lip until it bleeds, but you won't notice until you wipe your tears with your sleeve and feel the sting of the sleeve on your lips. You will see the bloodstain on your sleeve, and then you will believe. Since the woman you are watching is your godmother and your mother's best friend, go over and kiss your mother as she weeps. Hug her and love her. Watch your mother's tears roll slowly down her cheeks. Watch them fall to her shirt. Watch the tears leave large circles on her shirt and on your shirt, since she has been crying on you as well. Watch the woman's teenage babies crawl on the bed beside her and stroke her hair as she dies. They pull the stringy blond hair sticking from her swollen white face. You will remember how thin her face was before, wonder if she looks healthier with her face filled out. You will start to cry again and try to hide it. Make sure you have a tissue in your hand so you won't have to keep wiping your nose and your eyes on your sleeves. Watch her girls lie beside their mama and hold her hand. She will be sleeping, and you won't want to disturb her, even though you know you can't since she is in a coma. You will want to go hug her and lie beside her as her daughters are doing, but you will resist. You will decide instead to sit on the end of her stark white bed next to her feet in the hospital's socks. The bed will sink as you sit next to her weak body. You will regret that you hadn't seen her more, even though you lived in the same city. You will regret

142

that you felt you should not lie beside her. That you felt that this time was for her daughters and not for you. You wonder if she felt like you were her daughter, and you decide that she probably did. You will hear her raspy breathing, and the tension will build as you wait for her father to arrive from Virginia. You will wish that you were in Virginia, instead of in this hospital room watching her die. You will look at her pale, blank face and she will look so small. And you will jump every time her breathing stalls, even though you know she is hooked up to a respirator. You will place your hand on her foot, and your father will place his hand on your shoulder, and you will suddenly be aware that your mother's crying has ceased. You will hear her strong voice out in the hall, arguing with the nurse, begging to let the family stay with her as she dies. You remember that there are too many people in the room. You will look around to see pleading faces looking longingly at the pale body lying limp in the bed. They wish that there was something they could do. There isn't anything. Your mother will exclaim that this woman will die today, and you will flinch as you hear her say this. You will take a firmer hold on her foot and lay your head on the bed next to her leg. You will whisper that you love her. Wish that you had told her while she was conscious. You will wonder if she can hear you. And you will cry as her daughters stroke her hair.

— Dorsey Seignious

Liberation

When the sun scattered itself upon the ceiling, Kaylis rolled over on her back and studied the lines between the sunlight. She threw back the covers, pulled her hair out of a ponytail, and flung the rubber band across the room. She opened the closet door, yanked dresses and jeans off their hangers, ripped and shredded them, and tossed them on the bed. She pulled a box of photographs and old yellowing letters from under her bed. In the drawers of the nightstand, Kaylis found a brown paper bag of rotten iris bulbs and a jar of dead lightning bugs and tossed them in the pile. Tugging on the fitted sheets, she tied a knot to secure the items and dragged the bundle outside. She surveyed oak trees and the fields of slowly dying grass. She walked and tugged on the bag until she decided to just roll it in front of her until she reached the drainage ditch. There, she turned around, took a step out of her shoes and away from the pile. She looked back, inhaled, and shoved it forward.

As she walked back, she felt the dust between her toes, rubbing the skin raw and numbing the soles of her feet. *"Where are your shoes? You didn't go outside without your shoes, did you? Did you?" She wasn't suppose to know. But you sat on the couch with your feet up, knees against your stomach, walked across the linoleum floor and the carpeted living room. One. Two. Three.* "Don't you cry." *Legs burned.* "You know better than to go outside with no shoes on." *But Mama. Four. Five. It's because I love you.* "You just gotta learn not to . . . not to go out with no shoes." She looked to the sky and saw a small sea of clouds, tumbling one behind the other, slight breaks in between. The sun had been shining, but where? Trapped in a web of leaves among the trees. Trapped.

"It's not good for you to be up there all alone," she whispered. Kaylis approached the oak tree and placed her bare, dusted foot into the throat of the tree. She looked directly into the sun through the leaves and continued to climb. *"One, two, three . . . nine, ten. Ready or not, here I come."*

"You can't climb as high as me."

"Can too, girl."

"Nuh-uh." Must go higher. She gonna get me.

"You too fat to be climbin' any trees."

"Yo mama too fat."

"Yo mama."

"Yours."

"Girl, you crazy."

"You." Maybe . . . She reached a point where the limbs began to thin, shook the branches until she could clearly see the sun. She smiled. *"You're it."*

Kaylis gathered up a pair of scissors and a towel and locked herself in the bathroom. She tossed the towel over the tub. Pulling the toilet lid up, she bent over the bowl and held the mouth of the scissors to the crimped edges, feeding her reddish hair to the jaws of the glistening blades. *Don't never cut your hair, you got that hair like your great-great-grandmother. They say she was a big red woman, like an Indian, and had long hair. Hair like them Indians. She was said to be a beautiful woman. That's how you got that hair. Don't you never cut that Indian hair of yours. Never.* She watched the strands disperse as they hit

145

the surface of the water. *I am the vine, you are the branches; cut off from me, you can do nothing.*

"You can do nothing," she said.

"Nothing," she repeated as a handful dispersed upon the surface.

As the blades crossed the back of her neck, their coldness sent chills through her fingers. She tugged on the handle of the toilet and watched the hair spin and twirl into an abyss; some strands stuck to the porcelain. She stood up and studied the red handle of the scissors. She inhaled a deep breath, held it in her throat, and struggled to loosen the screw. They would be useless, but they would be free. The screw popped out and the blades were two separate beings; one in the left hand and one in the right. She looked at them, recognized their isolation, and tossed them in the sink. She walked over to the bathtub and tore the curtain down, its plastic rings shattering and bouncing across the floor and in the metallic bathtub. Kaylis turned on the hot water and twisted the cold-water knob as she admired the steam that rose from the surface. She stepped in and slowly submersed herself. *I baptize you, in the name of the Father, the Son, and the Holy Ghost.*

"The Holy Ghost," she said as she resurfaced. The bath water rippled as the streams of water fell across her body. She closed her eyes and bent her knees and slipped down into the water. She didn't come up for air; instead, bubbles emerged to the surface. *You must have faith in Him. He is the Alpha and the Omega. He is Salvation.* She parted her lips and allowed the water to flow in, trickling into her lungs, into her stomach, into her blood.

From beneath her ocean, she heard ringing. The loud dong of corroded, distant church bells. Her eyes opened, but she lay there, staring into the ceiling. Stepping out of the tub, she reached for the towel and wrapped it around her. She glanced in the mirror and squinted, examining the water that formed droplets upon her skin. *Upon the back car window. When the inside was hot and caused her to sweat deep in the seams of her flannel pajamas and the toes of her socks. At least the heater worked this winter. In the middle of the night, Mama woke her up. Pulled her from the sheets, wrapped her in a wool blanket, and carried her to the car.*

"Kaylis, you all right? Of course not, all night you been coughing. Gotta get my baby to the doctor."

"But, Momma . . ."

"Yes, baby, I'm coming. Yes, gotta get you to the doctor. Hear the wheezing."

Don't wanna go back there. Can't go back there, Momma, they stick her with needles, pull blood from constricted veins.

"She hasn't been drinking water."

"Yes, I know, she can't keep nothing down. My baby's sick, think it's pneumonia. Her papa think ain't nothing wrong with her. But I know when my child is sick."

Papa? Momma, Papa's gone. Been gone . . . to work? Away? Said he was gonna come back . . . He didn't.

"We can't find nothing wrong with this child."

I know. But my momma . . . she's sick.

She retrieved one of the scissor blades from the sink and stabbed at the mirror; its silver glistened and slid into the drain. She plucked the largest piece out and blew her breath across it.

She drew spirals in the temporal fog with the blade as she walked back to her room. She squinted while examining the barren room. As Kaylis walked to the window, she let the towel fall to the floor. Before she approached the window, she bent down and placed the blade and the mirror piece upon the towel. She closed her eyes and pulled the curtains down. The metal rod bent, snapped, and fell in two pieces on the floor. There she stood before the open window.

A feeling came over her, of eyes staring down her neck, creeping down and over her shoulders, around her waist and into the small of her back. *Eyes. One. Two. Three. Doctors. Counting the scars, blackened scabs. Touching them with rubber fingertips. Tracing them with alcohol-covered swabs that burned the open skin; its vapors burned my eyes. Four. Five. She hit her. Swollen cheeks, black and purple.*

"What happened?"

"*I don't know.*" *But don't touch . . .* She wrapped the curtains around her, allowing them to form a train behind her. She bent down and retrieved the blade and the mirror. She looked down at her arm, felt the blood pulsating against the walls of her veins and arteries, moving into her heart, deepened to holes in her stomach, swelling in the whites of her eyes. Painting her eyes pink. Tears drained onto her face, down under her chin, around her neck, following the path of her throat. She swallowed and felt it throbbing down into her stomach, dispersing into her blood. Blue and green, untouched by air. Untouched, she thought. There was not enough time for it to be exposed, revealed. She inhaled and closed her eyes.

"*Where were you going? Never in my life have I seen such dis-*

respect. Oh, but you want to run? Go on, run. Outside without your shoes, but you better not come back. Are you going?" One. Two. *"Look at me."* Three. *"No more running?"* Well . . . Four. Five. *"Of course not. Don't you cry in front of me. None."* Held glass to pursed lips. Half empty or half full? Never half full. *"Get away from me . . . you?! Never will I accept . . ."* She drew the mirror across a bluish-green vein that flowed into her hand. It was meant to be free.

— Tamara Butler

Feeling California

My brother and I grew up on the sandy shores of Laguna Beach, nestled in the cliffs of the California coastline. On Sundays our family traveled to the ocean in a Volkswagen camper that trudged slowly up the hills, climbing through the sun-drenched valleys and past the migrant workers who rented themselves out as laborers and sold strawberries. I never quite caught the contradiction of this situation — we with our eggs Benedict–filled stomachs bulging out of our little designer swimsuits, and they stealing a strawberry every now and then in their hand-me-down overalls. My mother always bought their strawberries, though, her blond hair rustling in the wind as she listened through their thick Mexican accents. They smiled at her as if she were a princess; their dark brown eyes gazed through sunburned skin at her pale complexion.

After purchasing the strawberries and turning to walk towards our van, my mother swayed as the Mexican men stared. The taste of sweet candy dribbled down my chin, and when I was finished eating, my mother always wiped my face clean with her paisley handkerchief.

With red-stained hands holding beach buckets, Matthew and I stormed out of the van and ventured down the steep steps to the sandy beach below the cliffs. My mother and father were left behind with chairs and picnic baskets clutched between their torsos and chests, laughing and meandering their way to a shady spot of beachfront. Matthew and I splashed for hours in the ocean. And when we built sand castles in the damp ground close to the water's break, my mother gazed at us, her knights in shining armor.

I peered back at her across the dimming blue sky. Her hair lay wet against her face, bringing out the shadows of her cheekbones, high beneath the glimmer of her keen-eyed stare. The outline of her nose sensualized her striking profile, and I never again wondered why my father fell in love with her. The mouth of her narrow-shaped face, encircled by a layer of maternal fullness, shone with beauty, warmth, and love.

She would call us to her when the sky turned pink with night light. At dusk, when the sun fell into the ocean, she always made splashing noises that sizzled as the orange flame touched the horizon. As a child I always wondered how warm the water got out where the sun touched down, and I wished, shivering in the cool air, that I could sink into that distant, sizzling ocean bath. Before leaving the beach my mom would shake our heads to get the sand out of our hair, and as we drove back through the valleys and hills to our home, she brushed my hair gently with a comb that smelled of roses.

The scent of roses still evokes memories of days without worries, without frowns. In my mind we were the royal family that traveled through the mountains, with our tummies full of hollandaise sauce and strawberries, thinking that living meant weekdays in swimming pools and Sundays on beaches. I never saw my mother frown in California; I never saw her cry one tear or lower her head. I never thought she was unhappy.

In the humid heat of the following August we moved across country in our Volkswagen van. The van struggled like a warrior to crest the Rocky Mountains. I wanted Laguna Beach back, my mother with the princess smile, and that sizzling sun that heated the ocean at the horizon.

We settled in Pennsylvania a few weeks later in a suburban neighborhood filled with Porsches and Jaguars. Our Volkswagen van didn't quite meet the standards of our neighborhood's expectations, but my mom was the prettiest mom on the block, probably the prettiest in the whole neighborhood, so cars didn't matter. On the day we were to move in, my mom ended up locked out of our house. She sat for hours at our neighbor's house, listening to how Catholic schooling was the right route to go and why public schooling would probably end in disappointment. I pictured my mom smiling noncommittally, with a grudging sympathy for such a sheltered view of life. This was not the education she wanted for us. My mother saw Catholic schools as havens for narrow perceptions and rigid thinking, hardly an environment of academic stretching and emotional stimulation.

If laboring up the hills of the Rockies, barely making it to the top, wasn't a sign of the difficult struggles moving would impose on us, then getting locked out on the first day was. My mother's happy smile of my childhood on Laguna Beach had quickly grown tired and drawn. She seemed unhappy and unsatisfied, as if she were living behind a wall where all her dreams were too far away for her to see anymore. The cold winters of Pennsylvania froze her smile and divested her of the pale glow that had shone so brilliantly in the California sunlight.

I saw in her eyes her longing, her sadness; I realized life wasn't Sundays on the beaches and weekdays in swimming pools. The coldness of our pretentious neighbors driving around in flashy sports cars hovered over our house, and the frigidity began to fill in the cracks and seep through the windowpanes.

In the depth of that crushing first winter, shortly after my grandmother had passed away, my grandfather was diagnosed with cancer. I knew my mother's heart was breaking clear down the center; as if to confirm this, a doctor's examination found an abnormal heartbeat, a prolapse. I wanted to take my mother back to the sunny weather and make her a glass of rose-scented tea, a plate of freshly sugared strawberries, and ask her to tell me what really happens when the sun goes down.

The stories of where the sizzling sun sets were only the beginning of my mother's ability to disguise realities. She had a way of hiding her pain like an actor can hide his true persona. I never knew if she was really happy or just saying she was to please me. She began to run constantly and lost a good bit of weight. Her thin face became more chiseled, more model-like — certainly different from that of the mommy I used to know, the one who ate eggs Benedict every Sunday before going to the beach. In fact, she started modeling for an agency in Philadelphia and quickly became the mom of many facets, the superwoman, the wonder mom. She taught Montessori to screaming, spoiled toddlers; she modeled on her days off; she ran marathons on weekends, kicked butt at Tae Kwon Do classes on weeknights, and still had time to transport my brother and me from school to soccer, soccer to swimming, and swimming to Tae Kwon Do. When we drove around, I noticed that she tilted her head slightly downward as if she were praying, except I presumed she was only dealing subconsciously with the pain she felt in her heart. I think life covered her sadness in busyness, and her frowning face was attributed to stress or, more politically correct, determination.

When she turned her head towards me, I realized that the mysteries of my mother's life lie in her eyes. She covers those mysteries well behind bright blue oceans of years of memories. Nowadays her walk is sharper and quicker than it was in California, distinct like a soldier, but sometimes with the swoopy hips of a New York actress. She built a temple out of her body of muscle and tendons to strengthen her heart. Her arms are well defined, and in the definition of her body I see that she is suppressing the pain of so many stories untold; the strength of her temple holds in its secrets.

I cannot pretend to know what pains her so. I only know that moving across country, that changing our lives, inspired something sad in my mother. I know that she mourns the loss of her parents deeply and yearns so often just to hold her mother's hand for one moment longer and tell my grandmother how much she needs her. I know that she feels the world does not appreciate everything she has sacrificed to be a good mother, one who not only rears a family but raises the beauty and value of the community in which she lives. Her days spent stretching canvas for an elderly artist and baking cranberry bread for the local soup kitchen somehow do not fulfill her as she once expected to be fulfilled.

These are only my ideas and speculations on why my mom could have grown unhappy, and I am beginning to realize that it might not have to do with California or moving. I don't want to go back to the smiley California mother of long ago when the world was simple and oceans in the distance seemed to sizzle. Now I know that the ocean isn't sizzling in the distance: The sun doesn't touch the ocean. The air in Pennsylvania does get warm in the summertime, god-awful hot, and that is good enough. Our pedantic Catholic neighbors can drive their Porsches and Jaguars and preach their private-school lingo. My mother will still send us to public schools and stand proud in her decision. My mother is a warrior. She has endured. She is no rich and spoiled beauty without any cares in the world. She is a survivor, and I love her as much for the frowns she shows as for the smiles she hides.

As I look back on the days when she stared peacefully into the calm of a California sunset, the vivid colors surrounding her whole body, I realize that happiness is a feeling that she can bring with her and have for the rest of her life. It is not one sunset over a blue-waved, crashing ocean. It is not one glimpse into the beloved's eye. It is not one car ride, tummy full and peaceful. Happiness is a moment, just as California was a moment in my mother's life. It will come around again; she will feel California.

— Stephen Fritsch

Reconstruction

My older brother, Karl, is visiting for the holidays. Among his scanty luggage — he is as practical as our father ever wanted us to be — he brings a few old photographs and scattered papers of Dad's. I study them behind closed doors, when both Karl and my mother are out, though Mom's reaction may well be no more than a passing "Wow," and Karl wanted me to see it all. Pulling the mess out of a plastic Radio Shack bag, I begin my search, feeling nervous and very intrusive. A search for what, I'm not sure. Maybe for my past, for my origins, for my parents. I don't know.

The photograph is dated New Year's, '72. This is eight months before they were married. They're at home — a sign on the wall reads CALIFORNIA MARIJUANA INSTITUTE. My father, shirtless, in jeans and a belt, is down on one knee, staring into the camera matter-of-factly, with a trace of a twenty-three-year-old's idealism. His dark, unwashed hair is tucked behind his ears and he's grown a young-thug mustache. In a fist, he holds the end of a white rope, to which is attached my mother, the cord a choke collar about her neck. She's down on all fours, her long blond hair falling around her shoulders and framing her face. Almost forcibly, she smiles the widest of grins. They both flip off the camera: my father quietly, reserved in this instance, and my mother raunchily. The photo is a touch out of focus and a pinhole at its top suggests that, for a time, it had been tacked up somewhere.

Staring into the picture, scowling a bit and mouth agape, I try to see them, understand *them*, the people they were, the type of girl she was. She was a Methodist, that was important to her and her family; she was the type who didn't have a boy in her bedroom till he was her husband. I suppose that was too long ago. I think, this photo is after her carny days and before now. Try to access the personalities of those times, try to forge a blend, a hybrid of the two, to make up a character to fit this photo girl who was soon to be a wife, then a mother, then my mother.

Dad, on the other hand, is the same person. Though I haven't seen him in years, he's always been the cocky adolescent in this photo. What more is there to say? He's to blame. Moving on —

A portion of a letter — never sent — of my father's to an old friend of his, dead of an overdose. Written while living at the house on Lynn Street, 16 Nov. 1976.

> *I have no kids, but I'm married to a neat blond (who is a distant cousin of mine) that I met on the carnival. We've two dogs (Pepper and Harold) and a cat (who's not bad, for a cat). We're happy, but thinking hard about the fastest way to make a million dollars, because I don't like to work.*

No kidding. That's why she left him. He wouldn't work. And add "pompous intellectual" to "cocky adolescent." That stuff about being cousins, whether it's true or not, is just like Dad. Throw it in there because it sounds interesting, sounds like he studies this stuff, like maybe he went to school, or is going to school. In truth, he's a dropout. He quit everything he ever started, walked away from it, maybe regretted quitting, but still, he walked away. He's a loser, though I hear he was quite charming.

My big brother's second Christmas: 1979. My parents stand with my mother's brothers and their wives. Each woman holds her firstborn; my mother holds Karl, clad in tennis shoes and a green parka. His white-blond hair is swept to either side of his brow, furrowed in a worried stare. My mother has gained some weight but is smiling: She looks happy. Behind her stands my father, in a blue T-shirt, jeans, and work boots, wearing the slightest of smiles within a five o'clock shadow. His hair is cropped short, unbrushed, and this is the leanest I've seen him, suggesting the height of his crank days. He is handsome nonetheless, and his features are reminiscent of an occasionally resurfacing military school education. He hardly looks like the high-school dropout he is.

The house on Lynn Street is difficult to reach. The street itself dead-ends at either end so we drive around until we find an entrance by a cross street. I peer at each house along the road, wondering which was ours, but Mom drives straight along. The cracked and patched concrete dissolves into scattered gravel and potholes as we climb an increasingly steep hill. The ride is rough. Mom gestures wildly to a structure along the side of the road, while trying to control the car. The house is burned yellow with dirty white trim. A dusty pickup sits on blocks in the driveway. Eight or nine concrete steps lead to the high porch where a window is visible. Through untamed trees, I see venetian blinds hanging crookedly. There's nowhere to idle, much less park, so Mom backs into the driveway to turn around and then speeds back down the hill again. I see the house for only a rough-and-tumble second.

1986 — My parents are divorcing. My mother makes Karl and me clean our room and I cry. Maybe because my parents are divorcing, maybe because I don't want to clean my room, probably both. I call my father's apartment, remembering his instruction to call him whenever I wanted to, ask him to come and get me. He comes right over, takes me, and asks my brother if he wants to come. My mother, wearing more weight, stands at the door, my brother at her side, my father and me on the porch. My father poses the question, speaking in a seven-year-old's voice. Karl shakes his head, puts his fingers in his mouth, and hides behind my mother's leg. Perhaps my mother looks triumphant. My father and I ride away and he begins to cry. He asks me for a towel on the floor of the car and I hand it to him. I watch him wide-eyed as he wipes his face and cries.

I'm eight and my father's daughter. All three of us are dressed practically, in T-shirts and jeans, my long hair tied back in a ponytail. We each carry a sack of groceries aboard my father's boat and my brother goes first. Dad tells me matter-of-factly, "You'll never be beautiful, Lenora. Pretty, maybe, just keep your tummy flat. But never beautiful."

I nod sensibly, because I don't care. Stuff like that shouldn't hurt my feelings, it's just the way it is.

God, I wish I could have been there. Really been there. It's so removed now, I can only watch while I relive the memory, watch Dad and me walk aboard and he tells me that. I want to run up and save that girl before she hears anything else out of his foul mouth. Want to tell her she doesn't have to listen to it, don't believe it, value yourself, run away anywhere from that man. Don't trust him so blindly.

Nine years later, I haven't seen him in four years. In my mind, my father is an old man, without family or roots or anything permanent. Pathetic. And I don't pity him because, just like he's walked away from everything else, he's walked away from me. Now, riddled with illness, he wants to meet again. To redeem himself, to try to fix the biggest mistake of his life, to relieve some of the guilt I hope he suffers from, to try to convince himself he could've been as good a father as he wanted to be. That he could have if only the circumstances were better. He was an innocent victim of circumstance.

So we go to see him, Karl and me. And God he looks awful, though — isn't it strange? — he is bigger than I remember him. First thing he tells me is, "By God, you're a beautiful young woman." I smile, thank him, look at the ground, kick the shit out of him in my mind, and scream that doesn't he remember anything? He goes on and states his typical bullshit: His estranged family is unnecessarily paranoid, he's as strong as a twenty-five-year-old, he's teaching himself German, et cetera.

Then he leads his own conversation about some Nazi philosopher and an American cover-up — who is the paranoid here? I want to scream in his face, but I sit politely, listen to his pseudointellectual drivel. Eventually, he brings up Mom and the D.A., how the system is screwing us, how it's preventing him from supporting his kids. He offers to send money, once we're both in college and on our own. I avert my eyes, blink hard, think about the years of missed child support. Try not to yell at him that he's a fucking screwup and that I'd never take his goddamn money. Later, as we part, he puts us in the position of reassuring him on his role as father. "It's all right," we say, "it's the past." He says something about wanting to have raised us on a ship in the South Seas, "If I'd had my druthers." Sure, Dad, I placate, want to get the fuck out of that place as soon as possible, away from Dad, never want to see him again, the miserable bastard. He wants to stay in touch. Talk regularly. Get to know us.

Karl and I drive home in silence. I decide, I saw him again, I gave him another chance, and I'm still not interested in seeing him. And now that I've seen him, met him, I can say that he *is* a pathetic, dying old man who is as stupid and backward as he ever was. He doesn't deserve my time. Nine years later, I'm telling myself I can turn away, I don't have to listen to him. I'm worth more than that. Dad walked away from everything he ever started. Maybe as he walked away he said to himself, "Gosh, I wish it didn't have to be like this." But that doesn't make up for it. He took a passive part in everything's destruction, ignored it as it fell into disrepair, then blamed someone

161

else when they finally took care of it. Like his marriage. Like his education. Like his children. Now Dad's walking back to us, wants to repair it, the relationship. Karl says I should be flattered, that this is the only thing he's ever walked back to. I say let him die alone. You can't repair an upbringing.

— Lenora Yerkes

Breathing Under Water

My parents never argue
Instead they sit side by side
On the couch, not touching
The television always on
Communicating something
They must have forgot

The evening news
Reflects in my dad's
Blue irises, as my mother
Sits folding laundry
Her small fingers running
Along the hem of the shirt
He bought her for Christmas

Watching them, I remember
The time I was pushed under water
In the neighborhood pool
I could see something else
Just above the surface
That I could not reach

My lungs ran out of air
And my arms began flapping
Like a drowning bird
After a minute, I realized

How normal it felt
To be deprived of oxygen
And I wondered if I could live this way,
Just beneath the surface
Forever
Breathing under water.

— Lindsay Greer

Going Back

And when I've had enough of this I take myself to the house with the broken door in the place where no one lives. The shadows here break through the windows in a thousand tiny patches, all patterned after trees whose branches push their way between sun and the glass so that the leaves stain my face on the other side. It makes me think of the simple things — how nice it is to be where people do not go anymore, where they do not rub off their lives. But from all that time ago, the things they used to tell their lives still remain. I see it in the rusty chain that hangs just inside the door. They are links of humanity tying those ghosts of the past to my own live hands. I know this as I fold the burnt metal across my knuckles and try to see the way we worked before something like a machine. This was when the air was clear and you could breathe without pausing in between, and when you let go of the breath, nothing filled you but the dust of yourself. I can taste that dust when I open my mouth in the rooms. It reeks with the forgotten, that which has not been stirred for years, so I feel lucky to swallow it all down. It has to be the deepest thing I have ever known.

Without anything like electricity the light fades fast from these rooms, but not before shining orange down the walls. It is that same sun that set here every day since the beginning of time, and may be the thing that has changed the least. If I could go back in time and space then I could still feel it on my skin, burning through in the same power it burns me now. It has spread its light over the fields out back, keeping them going and growing while all through the same years, this wood, this man-made house, has slowly gone the other way. It crumbles beneath my fingers in bits. I suck a weathered-wood, soot-covered finger, and taste 1900 or before. The ash trails gray from my mouth when I pull away.

That point when I finally lose all visibility, I must stumble out back to the fields. The grain keeps on going to the point of infinity and back; each fine, silk-tipped stalk dipping in the bare breeze, swaying and crashing into my side like bodies without control or without care. It makes me want to run, so I do, and the light is just right. It is barely making it here to me, but I am taking it for all it is worth. I go until my lungs feel ready to burst, then fall as if I am the last being on this earth. I have the scent of the world's every blossom coming at me a hundred miles an hour, and I imagine that the scent is created just for me. I breathe honeysuckle, breaking forth in stage of bloom or decay, and the scent of water running off. Like a Greek goddess indulging in my nectars, I inhale and ultimately am fed. Why aren't these flavors among the most desired in the world, right up there with caviar and escargots? Those stuffy ladies and stiff gentlemen at their dinner parties just don't know. The things they pick from the tines of a fork could be knocked clear off the table if they could only learn to take one deep whiff and be filled. Too much anymore, we are looking in the wrong places. Few have discovered the flavor of these dandelion roots. It is juice and then more, clear through the green. I smile a root-toothy smile and laugh at what they are missing.

When the moon slips in through the black, I am ready for it. I admire glimmers on my arms and the white reflections down the backs of my legs. The light creeps in as quietly as the crickets with their minuscule voices, sounds that I do not even notice until the crescendo has reached a near-deafening roar. Those tiny teeth, tiny forelegs grinding away, I can picture each one watching me with its beady eyes as I stumble to see beyond my own steps. Like they are packed inside my cells, I feel a tremor to explode with the noise. I could burst from my very skin like a twisted insect and crawl off to a new life — if only I did not have these places to go and deadlines to meet. Could it be that, all along, as we've so selfishly assumed we rule as the highest species, could it be that those microscopic critters, and even the birds, are laughing at us? Well, they can always fly away, but my arms do not even rise that high, so surely they must have one on us. Okay. I am willing to share. But wouldn't it be nice if they could teach us to find our wings and lift to the breeze?

If I stop to think my dreaming and my wandering are for nothing, I'll go crazy. You just have to keep on going back to that place deep inside that often calls but so rarely is answered. To take one minute and remember that there is more than machine and a hectic schedule, and simply pause a breath on the five A.M. dew. Step across it barefoot for once, to feel the chill clear inside your bones. It is like eating snow or digging into the dirt so deep that it clings up under your nails for days. It is the things the people of this house must have done once, before a time of gears and grinding. I bow my head to them, everyone who had the strength inside to find life and live it from this sky and this ground alone. If I could go back there, I would, so I could learn to appreciate what we so often take for granted, or so often do not care about. I would eat carrots right from their backyard and plow the soil in line with their strong backs. I would close my eyes every night to the whitest moon and feel the presence in my sleep. I would smell rain coming off wet bark. And the last thing I would hear each night before I went to sleep would be a light wind touching down through the fields and into my heavy head.

— Megan Shevenock

Hazelden

Hazelden, the packets said. *Hazelden.* All that came to my mind was Hazel from *Watership Down* and the Rabbits' Nazi warrens, but Hazelden was supposed to be the best treatment center in the U.S. *How do you measure that, most substance-free people!? Oh god this is a mistake, you can't be serious. I, Edith Eustis, am going to go to a place called Hazelden and spend my holiday learning to accept, heal, and understand? Why don't I just go smoke or drink something, then maybe I'll fit right in! The Family Program, what rubbish! I don't even want to see Mom, she can just stay there, we're getting along fine without her!* And then I realized that I was being the self-centered teenage girl that everyone expected me to be. That was not what I wanted.

We (my dad and younger brother Peter and the non-descript middle age driver) arrived at the entrance of Hazelden about an hour later. We were in Stixville, or more precisely Center City, Minnesota. There was no city that I could see. All I wanted was to go to the Mall of America and get the hell out of Minnesota. We drove down a winding road through acres of woods and passed lots of barrack-like buildings (I then acknowledged the fact that there would be no room service) and turned into the driveway of a slightly pleasanter looking building. There was Mom, cigarette in hand. When did she start smoking? *This is good, out with the old addiction and in with the new!* But I put on my happy face and gave her a huge hug, gushing unimportant trivia about my life in the past month.

She looked much the same, no visible changes of the workouts she had promised or the not drinking. Was this some sort of New Year's resolution that was quickly forgotten with a single afterthought and shrug of the shoulders? She looked exactly the same as when I had last seen her, olive green pants with a v-neck, button-down, yellow-and-green-plaid shirt tucked into her ridiculously high trousers.

She smiled and then informed us that visiting was almost over, so we had better hurry. Visiting — this is my mother, and she is not in a mental institution! I went over to her section and met the women in Dia Lin. They were busily stuffing their faces with popcorn while watching some Kevin Costner action flick on cable. They had cable!?! So much for getting in touch with the inner you! All the women were really nice, though — and they all seemed happy to see me. I hung out at my mom's dorm for a while (I call it a dorm because they all seemed to have such a blast together) and then went back to the Family Center.

My brother and I went to bed (we had to share a room) and woke up early the next morning; I should say *I* woke up early and went downstairs. Early at Hazelden is different from early at other places. Seven-thirty was check-in when the counselors or "leaders" called everybody's name, only a first name, and told us what we would be doing that day. Then it was off to breakfast, then morning check-in, lecture, small group discussions, and then lunch. Which was then followed by break until four, one of the twelve-step discussions, small group discussions, more break, dinner, after dinner "all-campus" lecture (one of the only times that guys and girls from the programs were in the same room together), and then freedom till the next morning.

There are a few important details of my personal experience the first day that I have left out: One, I got my Hazelden mug with Edith E. written in blue marking tape on the side, and two, I cried in a room full of strange men.

My mug was received my first morning when they oriented all the new people who had come the night before. They called out our names, only our first names, handed us some information and some forms, and gave us our mugs. *Mugs, how odd is this*, I thought, but over the next few days my mug would become in some way my most private thing, my individuality. Your mug is the one thing you really do not share with other people. That and the fact that many of the addicts and alcoholics in the center found drinking vast amounts of coffee helpful made the mugs a very good idea.

Now, crying in a room full of men was a little bit more complicated than getting my mug. It started with morning assembly. In morning assembly the group listened to a passage from a book or essay, and then we went around the room saying how we felt or related to this passage; but before doing that we all said our name, and what our family member's addiction was. I was less than thrilled, as if I was going to say, "Hi, I'm Edith, and my mom is an alcoholic," and then share my thoughts with these people. Yeah, right. I had to keep myself from laughing. But people did do it, every single one, and yes, you could pass if you wanted, but as many people know, when I have the opportunity to talk and have people listen to me, I do. So I did. With my blood pounding in my ears (no kidding, a bit like a first kiss), I said those few words that you see on Lifetime's made-for-TV movies: *Hi, I'm Edith, and my mom's an alcoholic.* No fireworks went off, nor did I feel suddenly liberated, but the one thing that amazed me — though I still had the wish to burst out laughing — was the response, "Hi, Edith!" said by almost everyone in the room. I had never felt like such an idiot.

Let me explain a few things about the Family Program. It is made up of family members as well as addicts and alcoholics further along in the treatment, and this made a world of difference. Getting to hear from both the family members and the addicts was much more informative than having family members, who were all confused by this phenomenon, bitch and relate their stories to one another. Imagine, if you will, a room full of teenagers discussing whether they should be allowed into an R-rated movie or have homework and you will have a pretty good idea of how effective it would be with just family members. The other two major things about the Family Program are that, one, it is the only unit besides rejuvenation that has guys and girls in it, for it is generally believed that drying out or detox is much more effective without sexual tension. In some ways it was like being back in seventh grade — totally separate, not talking, but still desperately trying to catch each other's attention. The second is that my brother and I were the only children (Peter twelve and me fourteen) in the whole of Hazelden.

After morning check-in we listened to a speaker, a woman whose husband's untreated alcoholism had subsequently contributed to the family's unhappiness and their daughter's abuse of substances. It was not so much the situation but how every person in the room could relate to it that affected everybody. After the speaker was finished we broke into small groups, in which I was never in the same one as my family, another wise practice that they had, since it allowed me, at least, to be much more open and honest. My small group, group number three, was comprised of Doreen, about six guys, and of course, me.

Most of the members of my group were addicts and alcoholics, with maybe two other family members in it. I had no idea at the time, but almost everyone in that room would greatly affect my stay at Hazelden and my future outlook on life.

When we got to room number three, it was just like any other room I had ever been in — any waiting room, that is. It was brown, everything in it was brown, there were no windows, only some chairs, a table, and a comfy-looking couch. The room was not depressing, however. It was rather like a big brown blanket in which you curled up and sleepily listened to your thoughts without digesting them. It felt like a place I would have to leave soon, something I had no desire to do. For most of my small group meetings I was in room three, and it became my refuge as I went in there with my mug and people whom I began to trust.

In small group discussions we essentially told of our experiences with the drug and how it affected us and then listened to the other people in the group comment about our experience and how they thought it affected us. This was the first place I really learned to listen to other people and to consider what they said about me.

I do not really know why I started crying, but I think it was the first time that I had ever really told anyone about how I was really feeling without putting up defenses or objecting to their understanding of it; and that is what made me start. Doreen had left early, so I was alone with six men, not teenagers or twenty-year-olds but middle-aged men, and I had the chance to learn now what they were learning in their thirties and forties, their fifties and sixties, and they were all happy for me. I do not think that I can understand why I cried, but I know that I did, and that afterwards I felt considerably lighter, more contented somehow. I had finally let everything in, and I felt like it was going to be fine.

On my last day there, we had a token ceremony where everyone who had finished the program asks someone who has made the most impact on him or her to present the token. I asked Kevin to give me mine, and yes, he was one of the six men in room number three who I had cried in front of, and he inspired the most hope within me. The token I received has the picture of a butterfly on it with its wings spread full; I keep it in my jewelry box.

I have a picture on my wall of a tiny kitten lying in an ancient Greek amphora; that is how Hazelden felt to me. As everyone said about Hazelden, it's a bubble. It is the most secure and the most vulnerable I have ever felt in my life (womb excluded). It has exposed me to people I would never have dreamed of meeting, wonderful people, who all took a wrong turn. I was lucky enough to see the consequences and learn from the people who made them. I no longer want to drink or smoke — it no longer holds any remote appeal for me. I have no reason to, only reasons not to; and I still have my mug on my kitchen shelf.

— Edith Eustis

A Poem in Three Conversations

Conversation I.

"You know," said the man in the black hat
to another man on the street.
"You're gonna die someday."

"I know," replied the pedestrian, "but I wish it wasn't so soon."

"Everything dies in the end," the man told him.

"Everything?"

"Even stars die."

"Oh," the pedestrian murmured sadly, looking down at the sidewalk.
An almost imperceptible drop alerted him to a change in weather.
"What happens then?"

"Well, it will be awfully dark, won't it?" the man in the black hat called
over his shoulder as he walked down the steamy street and turned into an
alley.

Conversation II.

"Why even live if we are just going to die?" the pedestrian sobbed,
sitting on the curb. His thin black umbrella provided
no respite from the rain.

"To love," said the old woman in the muddy white dress
selling newspapers.

"What?"

"We are given life so we may have the opportunity to learn how to
love." The dirty rain caused the newspapers to

bleed thin streams of ink down her dark hands.

"I'm not sure *what* you're saying," the man said, turning away.
He neglected to buy a newspaper.

Conversation III.

"Maybe," contemplated the newspaper woman, "we are worse off than
I thought." The rain, as if in answer to her contemplations, slowed to a
delicate drifting and finally stopped.

"There are horrors and wonders in the world," said the lonely beggar's
sign. "Who are *you*?"

"Terminal kindness,"
the newspaper woman said, dropping the change she had made selling
papers that day
into the cup under the sign.
She shuffled through the puddles of dark
clouds that clung to the pavement,
and met a man in a black hat at the corner.

— Christopher Schmicker

Faith

My mother works with a woman
who screams at God
as if he were an unfaithful lover.
My mother laughs,
but the woman looks to the sky
in case it has something to tell her.

I was an atheist by six,
when my grandfather died
and I could see
the clouds were too high and clean
to take him. I could tell
he went nowhere, but died
only a body
and a memory. My mother
didn't argue.

But now she is on God's side,
defending him
against the woman's demands.
I think my mother admires her, though,
the faith that is needed
to keep up an argument
with someone who never responds.

— Piper Wheeler

Meeting That Dude

The air is nimble and cold; it moves rapidly about me. Slim clouds swiftly slice the sky. I am ready for whatever shock the electricity in this night can give me. I pull the handle and push the passenger door open. Grounding myself as I touch the van's steel, a static arc sparks into my nerves, reminding me of the wintry disadvantage to a warm fleece layer. I close the door and stand next to Trevor under the dim light of the Taco Bell sign. His face is stolid and his eyes shift slowly around the lot.

"I don't see that dude here," he says flatly. "We're at the right place."

"Maybe he's late. . . ." I hesitate, trailing off. It is obvious that he is late — late or not coming.

"I wish that dude wouldn't do this crap." His face evinces none of the anxiety his voice does.

"Maybe he ran into traffic." Although I am here only because of my size, I wish Trevor were big enough to slap me for that comment. It's ten o'clock on a Friday night. There isn't a stationary car anywhere outside of a parking lot. The highway is a speeding race of blurs.

One of these ruby streaks, exhaust rumbling, angles into the lot, slows and rolls towards us. Its headlights make my eyes water, but I blindly follow the hazy corona as the truck turns into a parking space. Trevor lights a cigarette. The smell of lighter fluid from his chrome Zippo briefly precedes the acrid tobacco odor. He is slick. I hate smoking and never have done it, but the way he exhales is artistic. Girls admire it more than I do. There isn't another fifteen-year-old in the city with as many girlfriends as Trevor.

With a quick glance I see that he is mesmerized, but in a different manner than I am. Smoke plays around his face in a screen that camouflages his eyes. Only the blue in his pupils pierces the haze and analyzes the scene. With a practiced hand, he positions the cigarette between his lips. Its fiery tip glows brighter as he draws in. He exhales a sculpted cloud, and in doing so clears the air. He is calm, and I am not.

Drive-by shootings and glorified crime in rap excite me, but I have never actually been near anything illegal. Once I saw a drunk resist arrest. I watched the ruckus and told everyone the story, adding a few violent details for effect. My lungs filled to capacity, I think about the fact that I am in this story. Two men step out of the truck.

Scanning my memory for some reminder of what else might have happened tonight, I recall that Angela and I were supposed to see a movie. Dinner was going to be a surprise. I had saved enough to take her to a trendy French place uptown, the commonly mispronounced name of which escapes me. My plan was elegant: a nice entree, a salad, and maybe, if the waiter wanted a large tip, a crisp red wine. After the perfect meal I could have walked her to her front door to claim a kiss. On the way home, I would have listened to rap, popping potato chips and anticipating *Saturday Night Live*.

There were, however, a few complications in the throwing out of these plans when Trevor called. I had not yet taken them beyond conception, and Angela has no idea who I am. Besides, the thought of going to meet "that dude" rouses me more. All I have to do is look big — why he needs me — while he handles his business. I might try to seem tough, too, but now I notice the size of the thug across the lot leveling his index finger at us. I miscalculate my breath and my chest goes flat.

Trevor paints a cone of smoke onto the breeze and the man turns to stare at him. In a leverlike motion he ashes his cigarette into the wind and gazes back. Taking a drag, he dims his eyes' glare and says, "That dude still isn't here." Some smoke escapes his mouth as he speaks. When he is finished talking, he blows the rest out onto the atmospheric canvas.

The two men turn and go inside the Taco Bell, never to be seen again. My strained lungs relax and at the same time I try to say, "I thought maybe that was him." The words trip over each other clumsily; even the sounds I produce are an unintelligible jumble. Most people laugh and make of fun me. Cool guys always do that, especially ones who don't know me. Everyone thinks I am big and dumb. Trevor is the only person who calls himself my friend and really acts like he is.

I resume breathing and watch him twist the sole of his boot into the concrete, deftly extinguishing the cigarette butt between. He begins to drag his foot over the pavement, further crushing what remains of the tobacco and smearing it along in a line. Behind the final feathers of smoke a slight figure looms nearer, testing the ground with each step.

I stare at his face as my heart fires faster, and with a nod in his direction I signal Trevor. They exchange looks and begin a discourse that seems to be an introduction. The dry air burns my teeth as I suck it through them intensely.

He swings his arms and rocks his knees in gesticulation.

"You Trevor, the kid with the shit?" I search his skinny frame for some sign of danger or strength. What I find is a pale-faced boy. His eyes slide from me to Trevor and back again, staying fixed on either one of us for no more than a second. The waist of his pants is belted tightly to an area of his thigh no more than two inches above his knee. As he slides his hands into his pockets he crouches forward.

"Yeah, you Jason, the dude that paged me earli —"

Not waiting for Trevor to pause in his reply, the boy takes his hands out of his pants and waves his interruption. "Yeah, let's do this. Drive over to that street sign." For the first time his gestures serve a purpose; they point to a distant avenue.

Without looking at the street sign, Trevor deliberately removes a cigarette from his pack and rests it in his mouth. Staring intently ahead, he opens his Zippo and snaps the flint in one liquid motion. The yellow flame is taken into the tobacco, producing the anticipated exit of several wisps of smoke. Trevor cocks his head toward me and says, "That dude wants me to do this without even seeing the money."

I mark my calculated pause with an earnestly deep inhalation, then, "Maybe he thinks you're stupid." This time my would-be sophisticated dialogue serves a purpose. Digging nervously in his pockets, the frail punk steps back. He finds his money and counts it off, hands shaking, before he starts for the street sign. The air feels drier now than it did when he first approached us. I watch his slim shape's silhouette bob to his gait.

It's time to do it. Trevor unlocks the van doors and I pull the handle on the passenger side. As I touch the steel, I sharply miss the protection of the gun I do not have. Inside, I close the door and sit next to him under the dim light of the Taco Bell sign. Face excited, his eyes fix on the street sign two blocks away.

The engine turns over, drones, and Trevor rolls down his window to ventilate the cabin. As the car moves, smoke rushes out of his mouth into the night air. He drives his mother's mini-van towards the corner where Jason stands. At our only stop, I look both ways with him, breathing steadily, patterning my respiration. There is nothing to the right, but as I come to bear on the left, I make out a dark car. I exhale heavily and break the pattern. Both sets of eyes scan the parked vehicle. Its engine is not running, its light are off, and its driver sits staring at us, apparently alone. We are only two blocks from our destination.

Trevor pauses, shakes his head, looks again, and then continues on to Jason. A dense cloud of smoke plays over his lips into the darkness. He looks me in the eyes for the first time that night and says, "Be cool. That dude is going to pay me, and we're out of here." He hesitates, then, as an afterthought, says heavily, "Don't even get out." As the van pulls in front of the sign, I read the reflected letters LEMON STREET on the green metal plate.

His right hand quivers slightly as he lifts the shift into park. Sweat from his palms smears the lever as he starts to empty his pockets into the console. Finished, he snaps the cover shut and goes for the door. The handle clicks, and as the door opens, the white noise rushes in to fill my ears. Trevor swings his feet onto the pavement and slams the door, pulling from his cigarette all the while. An anxious breeze hums lowly in my sinuses, a sinister, low-pitched sound.

I cannot hear clearly the words exchanged between the two,

but I can see everything. Jason nervously jerks his arms as he stresses his phrases with obscenity. His vulgarity pierces the windshield as I watch Trevor proffer a plastic box from the depths of his hooded sweatshirt. The foul-mouthed boy fails in an attempt to grab the container with his hand, catching a fist with his face for his efforts. He shrinks to the sidewalk and scampers away. Trevor fumbles with his Zippo to light a fresh Marlboro.

A smile purses my lips. My panting stops. I swing open the door and jump out of the idling vehicle to congratulate Trevor on the well-delivered blow, but as I round the front of the van I freeze when I see what is pouring out of the shadows. Before I can focus, three men are around Trevor; three more are upon me. A confusion of grabbing hands throws me to the ground; I am overpowered by dim figures that push my nose into the asphalt. My gasping lungs shoot dirt into the blowing wind. Someone pats my rear, then takes my wallet. They turn me on my back and rob me completely. Keys, watch, even a pack of gum I have with me are taken. I know they will kick me, finalize their violence. I close my eyes, clinch my breath, and wait for the feet to come. They do not.

I let my air escape in a perplexed gust. Hearing footsteps retreating and car doors slamming, I quickly roll on my side and watch Trevor's van squeal around the corner, the strange car from the stop sign in the lead. Without a second wasted, I bolt over to find him. Now I am struck for the first time tonight by the realization of just how lucky I have been.

Trevor is doubled over, eyes closed. His legs impulsively try to walk even though he is prostrate on the sidewalk. He isn't bleeding, but he clutches his temples as he arches his back and struggles to breathe. He rights himself inch by paralyzed inch, then raises his head. Squinting, he shrugs his shoulders and wipes his hands on his pants. He has been completely outwitted, yet he smiles victoriously as he counts off on his fingers. "That dude took my phone, my pager, my watch, my lighter, my cigarettes, and the fifty dollars' worth of shit I was going to sell him. He missed the thousand dollars' worth I bought yesterday." Digging deep into his waistband, his eyes glow as he removes and touts his prized package. "Where's my mom's van?" Standing there in the streetlight, his tube glimmering with a sparkle once in his eyes, reality comes over Trevor, and he draws his first breath of alarm.

— W. Garner Robinson

The Silence in the House

The sun was setting by the time the Loneson family sat down for dinner.

"The days are getting shorter," said Mrs. Loneson. She sat primly upright, her posture flawless even in repose. "And colder, too." With one hand she slowly stirred her soup, the spoon revolving in patient, methodical circles through the thick liquid.

Mr. Loneson looked up briefly from his newspaper. "I suppose that's so," he replied. "That's what the days do at this time of year." His dinner lay untouched in front of him, the mashed potatoes slowly leaking gravy that ran in rivulets towards the green beans. To his left was set an empty place mat. His left hand lay on the place mat, palm downward, and with his fingers he beat out a steady staccato rhythm.

"The weather was beautiful yesterday," Mrs. Loneson said.

"I didn't notice."

"Well, it was. It rained in the morning, but in the afternoon the sun was out and the air was warm but not hot. It was a pleasant surprise for this time of year."

"It certainly sounds nice."

"Yes, I lunched with Diane and Elise and it was quite pleasant. Then I read on the porch all afternoon and that was pleasant, too."

"It sounds like it was pleasant."

"It was."

She stirred her soup, rotating the spoon deliberately. The house was silent.

"The weatherman said last night that today was going to be

just as beautiful as yesterday was. I saw him on Channel 2 on the ten o'clock news."

"Is that so? I didn't even get a chance to notice the weather today. I was tied up again."

"But he was wrong."

"What?"

"The weatherman, he was wrong. He said today would be as beautiful as yesterday but it wasn't. Today was cloudy, and when the sun came out it was cold."

"I'm sorry, dear."

"I had plans to visit the flea market with Elise, but it was too cold. I can't bear it when the sun isn't out. I read all day again and cleaned the house again and napped, but not well. It was too quiet to sleep well."

"I'm sorry, dear."

"Don't be sorry," Mrs. Loneson said. "It's not your fault I listened to the weatherman."

"Maybe tomorrow it will be good weather again."

"No. The good weather's passed us by, I don't care what the weatherman says. I don't trust him anymore, anyway."

The sun had flattened itself into a swollen oval hanging heavily on the horizon. The sky glowed a dull orange that gradually gave way to indigo and then violet, and where the sky was violet the first stars twinkled faintly.

Mr. Loneson stood up suddenly. He strode calmly to the window, newspaper under one arm, and closed the blinds.

"No, leave them open," said Mrs. Loneson.

"But the sun is right in my eyes," protested Mr. Loneson. "I can hardly see with it coming through at that angle."

"Please, leave it open," she repeated. "The sun is always so pleasant. It will be gone any minute now, and then it won't bother you anymore."

Mr. Loneson nodded. He resumed his seat and his deliberate staccato tapping. Mrs. Loneson stared at the kitchen floor and was dazzled by the glare from the reflection where the sunlight struck the tile. With one hand she stirred her soup.

"I talked with some people at the insurance company," Mr. Loneson said.

"What did they say?"

"They said they finally checked it out and that the car can't be fixed after all. It's totaled."

"We knew that months ago. We didn't need the insurance company to tell us that."

"They needed to make sure."

"I knew the car was totaled as soon as it happened. I don't need an insurance company to tell me I totaled my car when I'm the one who totaled it."

"It wasn't your fault," he said.

"I still totaled it."

"No, you didn't," he insisted. "None of it was your fault. How were you supposed to know the stop sign was down?"

"What else did the insurance company say?"

"It wasn't your fault. You know that, and so does the insurance company."

"What else did they say?"

"It wasn't your fault."

"Stop it."

"It wasn't."

"I'll scream."

"They said that they'll replace the car but only up to the value of the last one. We'll have to pay the rest."

"We can afford it now."

"It wasn't either of our faults."

He opened up his newspaper and resumed his fingertip cadence. "I looked through the classified section for you earlier today," he said.

"I'm not ready yet."

"I found some jobs that look interesting, that look like the kind of work you'd like."

"We don't need the money."

"I know we don't need the money."

"So I don't need to work yet."

"You don't need to work at all," he said. "You know that. But I think working would be good for you, would give you something to do all day besides worry about the weather."

"Maybe I like worrying about the weather."

"All I'm saying is that I think it would help you to do something worthwhile with your time. It's not healthy to sit around all day."

"I'm not ready yet. It's hardly been any time at all since it happened."

"It's been long enough."

"I'm not ready."

"You need something to get your mind off it, something besides how sunny it is or what the weatherman said last night."

"Don't tell me what I need! I need the sun."

"All I'm saying is that —"

"I know what you're saying."

"Well, exactly. All I'm saying —"

"I don't care what you're saying," she said.

"Okay. I understand," he said. "You just tell me when you're ready to work, and we'll find you something interesting to do."

"I'll tell you."

"You do that."

"When are you going back to work?" she asked, stirring her soup patiently and methodically with her right hand.

"I want to get back by eight, so I can finish up some of the paperwork before midnight."

"You're not coming home again tonight."

"Probably not. I have to be in at seven tomorrow anyway, and it'll be a late night. I'll probably sleep at the office."

"So you won't be home at all?"

"It's my work, dear, you know I have to."

"I know you have to."

"I have to finish up the paperwork, that's all, dear. Otherwise you know I'd be here."

There was a short silence. She stirred and he tapped and the swirling sound of her stirring and the staccato beat of his tapping only added to the finality of the silence that gripped the house.

"But can't you please just stay tonight, please?" she asked hesitantly.

"You know I can't."

"Please, just tonight," she said. "I've been cooped up inside all day, I can't take the silence, I can't take it with no one here, I need you tonight."

"But the paperwork, dear, you know I have to finish the paperwork by tonight."

"Please, just take this one night off, darling, please," she begged. "I can't take the silence again tonight. Not after being here inside all day with no sun."

"Tonight is the worst possible timing. I'm sorry, I — I simply can't tonight."

"Just this one night?"

"Not tonight."

A pause.

"Any other night, and you know I'd say yes. But not tonight. You know I wouldn't lie to you."

"I know. You have to finish the paperwork."

"See, you understand," he said. "You know I'd be with you if I could, if this was any other night."

"Of course you would."

"You know I would."

"I know."

"Good. But tonight I really can't."

"I know."

"Good. Now let's have a pleasant dinner, dear."

"Yes, let's have a pleasant meal. At least the sun is still out. At least I still have that much."

He nodded and folded up his newspaper. He placed it on the seat to his left in front of the empty place mat.

"Don't do that!" she cried.

"Do what?"

"Move it! Move the newspaper!" Her voice rose sharply. "Don't put it there as if that seat doesn't belong to anyone anymore!"

"It doesn't belong to anyone anymore," he said grimly.

"Don't you say that! It's still his seat, and don't you say otherwise. Get your paper off of his seat!"

"It's not his goddamn seat anymore," he growled.

"Don't you dare say that again!" she cried. "Don't say it!"

"It's not his seat! It's not! He's never going to sit there again, it's not his!"

"Shut up! Shut up shut up shut up shut up shut up!"

He snatched the newspaper off the seat and flung it across the kitchen.

"There, are you happy? It's gone, it's gone, you win, I moved it, it's gone."

"I know it's gone," she said quietly.

He squinted into the last rays of the dying sun and blinked quickly. His left hand crept back onto the place mat and the staccato rhythm began again. She was stirring her soup.

Dinner passed and the sun sank beneath the horizon until only the last faint rays of daylight were visible. Mr. Loneson finished his soup and made a dent in the mashed potatoes, then checked his watch, jerked to his feet, kissed his wife on the cheek, gathered his newspaper off the kitchen floor, and left to finish his paperwork. Mrs. Loneson sat alone at an empty table set with three place mats and two plates full of food. She patiently stirred her soup and stared at the kitchen floor tiles and listened as the silence in the house grew louder and louder until it roared with all the grief and fury of her shattered existence.

Suddenly she snatched up the TV remote. She pointed it at the television and roughly jabbed the power button. The Channel 2 weatherman appeared on screen, dressed impeccably in an Armani suit, every hair gelled perfectly in place, his burnished white eyeteeth glistening between smiling lips. It's going to be another beautiful day tomorrow, he promised, a high temperature of seventy-five degrees without a cloud in the sky.

Mrs. Loneson looked outside and watched the thunderclouds rolling in from the northwest. "It won't be beautiful tomorrow," she said to the television weatherman. "I don't believe you. I don't trust a word you say. It'll never be beautiful again. We've lost all that." She punched the power button and the television died abruptly.

The last vestiges of the sun sank behind the horizon and the violet color of night followed in pursuit and settled to the earth. The stars twinkled and the house was silent.

— Joshua Howes

A Boy Wakes Up with No Head

A boy wakes up with no head. Everything above his shoulders has disintegrated, dissolved, disappeared. The rest of him is all there, but around the neck of his green-and-blue-plaid pajamas he feels an unfamiliar nothingness, a void, an abyss, a gorge. Looking in the mirror, it seems to the boy that during the night an executioner, scarred and masked in the pitch-black, severed his sleeping head with a shimmering ax and stole away with it. As he examines himself for any strange lacerations, he remembers a story he heard about someone who was robbed of his internal organs, which were then sold on the black market. Nothing. He frantically searches for the missing body part in his room, which looks as though someone made a tremendous pile of semi-clean clothes, compact discs, floppy disks, zip disks, music magazines, sheet music, mechanical pencils, Kleenex, and paperback books and detonated a bomb under it, sending shards all over the place. Nothing.

He feels around in the black oblivion under his unmade bed. His frantic hands graze something round. They claw for it, trying to grasp the newly found orb of hope. Boundless joy erupts through him like an entire symphony orchestra playing in unison. *I found it!* he thinks to himself. *Now everything is fine!* The symphony crumbles — the once brilliantly shining brass twisted and warped, the strings snapped and frayed, the flutes, clarinets, and oboes clogged and choked — out of key, out of tune, out of sync. It is just a basketball.

"Where is my head?" he says out loud to no one. The clock

next to his bed reads 7:30. A half hour stands between him and a world of torment and angst. *7:31.* The clock taunts him. "I can't go to school like this." The boy, panicked, almost cries. Imagining the relentless, giggling girls, the fragments of whispered gossip, the epidemics of rumors, the embarrassment, the humiliation, the helplessness, he throws open his closet door. *Maybe if I wear stripes, it will be less noticeable,* he thinks, trying to muster some hope.

7:45. BREEEEE! BREEEEEE! BREEEEE! declares the boy's merciless clock.

"Honey! You might want to think about getting up!" calls his mother, a reminder of the certain doom that awaits him. The boy catches himself as he enters the bathroom and remembers: There are no slightly crooked teeth to brush, no face to wash, no mass of curly brown hair to check out. Everything is gone, cleared away. Every hygienic ritual is now archaic, out of date, obsolete, futile. *What's the point?* he wonders to himself, longingly.

After one last inspection of his tornado-ravaged room, the boy shoves a tome-like history book into his black backpack and heads downstairs to face his fate. "I set out your crunchy fiber twigs on the table. Be sure to eat them, sweetie, because I read that children who eat good breakfasts are thirty-seven percent more likely to be smart and popular," the boy's mother says from the kitchen.

"Uh, great," he murmurs, as if he were trying to speak through a white plaster face cast.

8:00, reads the kitchen clock, as if to say *Ha.*

*   *   *

"Good morning, everyone." The math teacher, wearing glasses with thick gray lenses like windows on an airplane, welcomes everyone in the forced amiable tone of someone about to present news of a natural disaster or tragic, shocking death.

"You will have only half the class period to complete the test. After that, you must put your pencil down immediately." He hands out the brilliantly white test packets. As the boy tries to complete the vicious math problems one by one, he feels embarrassed, humiliated, helpless. The second he had arrived at school, he knew how right he had been. Everyone had looked at him a little strangely, as though he had two slimy, green tentacles coming out of his skull, as if he were a freak, a weirdo. He could swear he heard two younger girls whisper, "There's that boy with no head," as he passed by, notorious, infamous.

The boy cannot concentrate, cannot focus on the test. It is as though he is swirling around endlessly in a whirlpool made of variables, cosine functions, exponential growth patterns, and trucks traveling towards each other at forty and sixty miles per hour, respectively. He looks out the window, which is covered with little raindrops like tiny sprinkles on a gray cupcake. Outside, the sky is overcast, gloomy, dismal. The clock on the classroom wall reads 9:15, seeming to say, *You must stay here for another seven hours. You have no head and everyone knows.*

Walking through the packed, crowded, rectangular halls on the way to the next class, no one says hi to him; everyone seems to stare straight on like gargoyles; no one even meets his eyes. *I don't even have eyes to meet*, he says to himself, mournfully. He feels he is a pariah, hated, reviled; a disgrace; an obloquy. Then all of a sudden, she appears at the end of the hall. She is sunny, dazzling, as though she could fit equally well in a Renaissance painting, among golden-haloed saints and beams of light shooting out of dark, powerful clouds, or on the cover of a teen fashion magazine. It seems to him that she emits a light glow, an aura like a small planet on a cloudy night, as she walks. He loves her shiny blue glasses, the way she crinkles her forehead when she's thinking, her slight accent that he can't place. As she passes by, his melancholy hopelessness seems to float away like a lost red balloon gliding up into a clear white sky — gone forever — only to return, tied to his wrist once again, the instant she disappears.

11:00. The clock face glares at him. To the boy, it is as though the entire high school is in on a diabolical, clandestine conspiracy, centered on his mortification, the destruction of his dignity, self-esteem, self-worth, and self-respect. It consumes his thoughts, eats away at him like drops of acid on a piece of white bread, sputtering, sizzling. It pushes out, overruns, conquers, annihilates any other sentiments but self-consciousness and fear. Then, from out of nowhere will appear the resplendent girl who will for a moment melt his murky fog, dispel his nebula of dread with her radiance and let rays of optimism beam through his mind like a laser show of happiness. *I'm going to talk to that girl*, the boy will say to himself and then realize, *Oh. I don't have a head.*

His day goes by like a snail climbing Mount Fuji. He walks around aimlessly through the day, finding solace in nothing; no peace of mind, no tranquillity, no Zen sense of oneness. He

197

stares at the never-ending lines of rain outside, the tan, worn tiles on the floors, the posters on the walls of women's rights advocates, football stars, inspirational, pastel-colored paintings of vibrant blue oceans and jumping dolphins, chaos theory fractals, eighteenth-century Romantic poets. During lunch, he sits alone, secluded, isolated, separate, detached, severed. He begins to come to terms with living a life of solitude, ostracized from civilization, condemned for failure to conform, never to make a connection again, constantly aware that behind his back there are always a few cautious, deliberate eyes transfixed on him, staring at him piercingly, the way they would at someone with one eye during a lesson about pirates. *I've already lost my friends*, he thinks, despondently. *My parents are probably the next to go. I am a monstrosity.*

Yes, you are. 12:30, the cafeteria clock appears to boom.

The boy jogs around the football field, soaking wet like a mop from the rain, and watches the heavily padded, brawny, stratified players slam into each other like medieval knights or pachycephalasaurs. A crowd of girls gazes fixedly at the displays of machismo.

5:00. See? Girls like pachycephalasaurs, not guys without heads, the clock tower seems to hiss at him.

OK, you're right. That's it. Just as the boy is letting go of his last shred, his last streamer of hope, she appears again, alone, standing in the rain. As the day has gone by, her glow has gotten stronger, more brilliant, more effulgent; the layers and layers of dreary, forlorn clouds have melted away, taking with them the boy's personal haze of inhibitions, premonitions, doubts, fears, defeats, and rejections. Tiny rays of light glint off her. Droplets of rain cling to her luminous glasses. It is as if they are meant to meet at this very moment — as if everything has a purpose, a point, a resolution. To the boy, everything is beautiful — he and the girl have made a connection, reached a junction.

"Hey," he says.

"Hey," she says, with a slight accent that he can't place.

She is not wearing a watch. He smiles. Somehow it does not matter that he has no head. They could both have no bodies, no form, no tangibility, no substance, just an existence in the endless rain.

"Would you, uh —"

— Alex Nemser

George Orwell's Writing Advice

Although many people believe that the evolution of language is beyond our control, this is simply not true. Anyone who has ever read my essays would have to admit that the English language is in a sordid state. This is not entirely my fault, however. I place much of the blame on society, which is crumbling faster than an Oreo cookie being run over by a turquoise freight train. Why is the train turquoise? I have no idea. I just added that word because I like how it sounds. And why did I use the word Oreo? It's because Nabisco is paying me to advertise their delectable cream-filled cookies. See how corrupt and decadent I am? This decadence obviously has an effect on writing. Just the other day, I ate a pint of Oreo ice cream and my writing became absolutely nonsensical. Come to think of it, I don't remember if it was Oreo ice cream or heroin ice cream, but you get the point.

Clearly, the decline of our language must have political and economic causes. Yet at the same time, these causes are caused by the decline of our language, which is caused by these causes. Are you confused? I can explain it better: Draw a circle on a piece of paper. Did you do that? Okay, now write the word "English" somewhere next to the circle. Good. Now draw an arrow from the word to the circle. Now put your pencil down and stare at the paper until you understand. Are you still confused? So am I. Damn, this analogy isn't really working out, is it?

What I'm really trying to say is that we can make our writing and our language better by eliminating bad habits. Some of these habits include drug abuse, indecent exposure, homicide, animal abuse, and belching. In any case, here are some examples of passages that demonstrate truly horrendous writing. I may refer to them later in the essay, but I might forget to.

1) *The quick brown fox jumped over the lazy dog.*

2) *See Dick! See Dick run! Run, Dick, run! See Jane! See Jane run! Run, Jane, run! See Spot! See Spot go! Go, Spot, go!*

3) *Each party shall, at its own expense, comply with any governmental law, statute, ordinance, administrative order, rule or regulation relating to its duties, obligations and performance under this Agreement and shall procure all licenses and pay all fees and other charges required thereby. Each party agrees to comply with all applicable federal, state and local laws, regulations and ordinances, including the Regulations of the U.S. Department of Commerce and/or the U.S. State Department.*

4) *Согласно распоряжению, органам исполнительной власти субъектов Российской Федерации, в которых осуществляется строительство метрополитенов, рекомендовано.*

Each of these passages has unique faults, but one thing is common to all of them: They make my essay look longer than it really is. Passage #1 is simply mind-blowing — it manages to use *every* single letter of the alphabet. You probably think I'm lying about that. Go ahead and count for yourself. I can wait. Are you back yet? See, I told you so. I'm impressed that the author managed to use every letter — even x and q, which are so unpopular that the other letters in the alphabet tease them and take their lunch money. However, despite using all of these letters, the author is obviously being vague and intellectually lazy. The whole scenario of the fox jumping over the dog is stated in such ambiguous terms that the reader does not even know whether the fox was eventually shot and skinned or not. What kind of writing would leave such crucial questions unanswered?

Passage #2 is not only ambiguous but is also repetitious, cyclical, circular, and repetitive. We are thrown into the middle of a smoldering love triangle among Dick, Jane, and Spot — but what information are we given about these people? The author tells us that they "run" and sometimes "go" — obviously sordid metaphors for unspeakably depraved sexual practices, but why should one resort to such convoluted linguistical denotation? The use of obscure and obsolete words such as "run" is a common characteristic of sciolists, misotramontanists, and gynotikolobomassophilics. Words such as this should be retired to the sabbulonarium, where they belong.

Passages #3 and #4 demonstrate the chaos and ugliness that result when one writes passages using too many foreign words. These passages are so convoluted and meaningless that they almost seem as if they were written in another language. Although using popular foreign words and phrases may add a certain *je ne sais quoi* to your prose, it indicates that you are too slovenly and degenerate to come up with authentic English writing. This is obviously *nicht gut*.

Clearly, the authors of these passages are too slothful to finish what they begin — their writing is convoluted, ambiguous, unclear, obscured, mysterious, uncertain, blurred, indistinct, hazy, confusing, and repetitive. Unfortunately, this *malaise d'écriture* is representative of much of the careless writing going on in the world today. I picked up a Chinese newspaper the other day, and I was shocked by how many foreign expressions were used. I could barely make out a single English word among all the boxes with squiggly lines coming out of them. Do you know what the triangular one with two intersecting lines is supposed to mean? I certainly don't. Indeed, some writers today are so intellectually indolent that they don't even bother to finish their paragr

In general, there are some simple rules that you should follow to improve your writing. First, don't use verbal false limbs. These tend to break, causing you to tumble off the tree. Let me tell you something, though: If you're too stupid to know that you shouldn't stand on false limbs, you should give up tree climbing and stick to writing. Also, don't use pretentious diction. For example: instead of saying "don't use pretentious diction," say "don't use big words" instead. Do your best to avoid euphemisms — replace "We fulfilled our objectives by pacifying the countryside" with "We blew up some folks just for the hell of it." This honesty will make it much easier for people to decide to fire you. Finally, never use dying metaphors. If you see a metaphor that is dying, drag it into an alley, finish the job, and then hide the body really well. Don't leave fingerprints.

The situation might appear desperate, but don't lose hope — I know exactly how to improve our writing! We should start by establishing a massive government agency to keep track of what everyone is saying and writing. Then we could cut out all the useless and decadent words from the language. Why do you need to say "good" and "bad"? Just say "good" and "ungood" instead. That's one less word to clutter your head. It adds up, you know. This is actually a really neat idea. I think I'll try to write something about it. You can't write on an empty stomach, though, so I'm going to run to get some ice cream first. *Au revoir*. Please buy some Oreos.

— Ilya Abyzov

An Open Letter to the College Process

Dear College Admissions Process,

I am writing you to request that you kindly give me back my will to live. It took many years of feel-good after-school TV specials and Dr. Seuss books to convince me that I could actually get somewhere in the world, that I could gain some modicum of success and acquire a fulfilling job and a home and a wife and 2.3 kids.

Thank you for proving Dr. Seuss wrong. "Oh, the Places I'll Only Ever See on Television" is more like it. You probably have some evidence to prove to me that Mr. Rogers is a pedophile, too, don't you?

It all looked so hopeful, too. All those years of elementary school getting A's without ever studying. That era of being widely recognized as the smartest kid in school. The adoring teachers. The proud parents. The nice framed awards. If you had told me back then that I was on my way to Harvard, I just might have agreed with you.

Then I came to Hunter College High School, New York's Capital of Low Academic Self-Esteem. I really thought I was special; I thought we were all special. Then I realized that year after year, the most popular trend at Hunter is believing that the best school you'll ever end up at is Apex Tech.

Not to say that refrigerator repair is a bad profession. I have many friends who are refrigerator repairmen. Okay, just one. And he's my brother's friend. When I was three (and already thought I was going to Harvard), my brother and this friend used to make me shoot milk out of my nose. But that's a different story. A very different story.

Anyway, back to why you ruined my life, College Process. So I was trying to make my way through Hunter, trying to kludge through all this coursework without having my hair go gray at the tender age of thirteen. And then this magical voice from above tells me that there's more to getting into college than doing well in your classes. Oh, no, that would be too easy. There are these things called SATs.

Now I have to tell you something about the SATs, College Process. We have a very bad relationship, dysfunctional at best. According to the SATs, I have the mathematical capacity of a chimp with a learning disorder. I'm going to be that kid taking SATs while there's snow on the ground and thrown-out Christmas trees are lining the streets. This does not make me happy, College Process. I like Christmas. That's my holiday. It was when I found out about SATs that I found out about Hunter's other great belief: Anything Less Than 1600 Means You're An Idiot. If your SAT score is more than a thousand and the second number isn't a six, don't even bother. And don't get me started on SAT2s, i.e., Another Way for The College Board to Take Away a Friday Night.

Which leads me to the Third Noble Truth of Hunter: If It Doesn't Have Ivy All Over the Walls, It Is Not a College. The old joke, "There's Harvard and then there's everywhere else," works very well at Hunter. Oh, sure, we know we won't get into Harvard. We even know that we'll probably end up at a respectable private university with a salad bar and free parking. We know we'll most likely get into a fine school where we'll be perfectly happy.

But we'll be bitter about it.

Now I'm not so sure, College Process. Good ole CP. I'm not sure if hating you is just the result of an odd Hunter tradition of believing that we're all going to crash and burn trying to get into college like a Ford Explorer before the recall. Maybe we're just paranoid. Maybe it's fun to think you're scum. Maybe all this academic self-esteem bashing is the only thing that's making us do any work at all. Then we'll get to college and realize it wasn't so hard at all and that we just enjoyed whining. Show me a Hunter student who doesn't whine, and I will show you a liar. Then I remember the Financial Aid application. And my hate for you returns.

Sure, there are easy ways out. The "Applications Process" for Long Island University involves going to their admissions office with your transcript. They decide whether or not to admit you While U Wait. Drive-thru college admissions. God, that sounds like a dream. Then again, LIU is in Brooklyn, yet calls itself LIU. That doesn't bode well for the academic quality of the university. But the Giants are supposedly from New York and have their home stadium in New Jersey. So there is a precedent.

But no, LIU isn't good enough for Hunter students. Despite our complete confidence that we are scum, we still want to go to schools that require endless amounts of paperwork. We want to be the kings of scum. While kids are out there going right from senior year to Starbucks, we whine and cry when we get into, ohmigod, OBERLIN!

We'll have no Oberlin bashing in this house, young lady.

We have the strangest perspective of the world here, CP. We all expect to go to college. It's not even something we think about. It's like we think it's our right to go to college or something, like all this work we did all these years has to lead to something, has to lead to some idyllic campus among green, rolling hills.

I'm just happy it's not leading to a Starbucks apron.

God, I feel so spoiled and privileged now. Sorry for the interruption, CP. You can go back to shuffling all of us snot-nosed academic brats around the world's campuses now. Forget I ever said anything.

Oh, and would you like whipped cream on that frappucino?

Sincerely,

Your Humble Overachiever

— Geoffrey Guesh

The Searching

I'd been searching for a poem for days.
I'd been searching for a poem
as girls search for lost dolls
and as lovers search for true love.
In the morning,
I would check under my covers
to see if I could find a sleeping poem
lost in the folds of the sheets.
Throughout the day,
I would slip my hands into the pockets of my jeans
in hopes that the crumpled knot
would be a chain of words
and not my silver necklace.
At night,
I would rub my hands along the bathroom mirror,
where I had found so many poems before,
but instead of dripping with a glistening stanza,
my fingers would come back dry and empty.
While everyone slept
I would crawl along the ground
and check between the cracks of the floorboards
for words that had dropped from tired mouths
and rested there.
And then, this morning,
I opened my mouth to moan with defeated frustration,
and out fell a shivering, heaving poem

wrapped in the dark chocolate taste
which had enveloped my tongue for days.
I took the new-born poem in my hand
and laughed at myself,
because all this time I had been searching the corners of the house
so diligently
that I had failed to notice
the familiar taste of written words
in the corners of my own mouth.
With the joy of a girl who is handed her lost doll
and the ecstasy of a lover who actually finds true love
I dripped the poem onto a piece of paper
and started the search again.

— Caedra Scott-Flaherty

alphabets

they are all so beautiful.
japanese is in quick yet perfect lines,
as though designed by some
woman or man who was
running out the door in just a few moments,
and as a sort of afterthought
jotted down a few letters,
not meaning to be elegant,
but somehow unable to help it.
hebrew print is formidable,
each smear of ink so meticulously placed,
as though hundreds of old men
argued for hours about each
broadening and kick of each line;
but the script undoes it all,
twisting itself into curves and softenings
in a seamless dance
to an eccentric beat.
arabic was created one day
by a powerful hand
skipping stones on immortal water,
most of the stones sinking,
leaving thick,
ink-laden ripples that bled into one another,
but others floated on top for a moment,
hard points above the gentle current.

greek is an odd collection of things
that happened when too many brilliant minds
tried to find the right symbols to capture
their exact thoughts —
it began patiently,
hands trying endless combinations
of strict lines,
but ended in a flurry of curves,
because the thoughts were simply
too ingenious to be held anymore.

then i turn to the roman alphabet
and see blank letters.
each character is too much just a symbol,
meaning nothing and
coming from nowhere,
its only purpose to stand for
this one sound.
i wonder if the greeks and japanese
think of it as something meaningful,
perhaps as the cracks in an eggshell,
or the folds in the dress
of a long-banished muse.

— Valerie Ross

Theme and Development
or, Sonata in the Form of a Burrito

"Hey faggot." The first movement of Johann Sebastian Bach's Sonata No. 1 for solo violin begins with a ripping G-minor chord, and these two words collide with my eardrums in the same jarring manner. I'm working at the taco joint just off the highway, and at this time of night I don't expect any customers except for the old Mexican with the white mustache who is poring over yesterday's paper in the corner. Tracing the stained white tiles on the floor to the door, I search for the source of this loud disruption, the words still ringing in the fluorescent air like the long, sustained note that follows the opening chord. My gaze falls first upon an oversized pair of sneakers, then faded green corduroys, and finally a compact body and German-looking face whose bilious blue eyes are staring right at me. He repeats the words, "Hey faggot," louder and more forcibly this time, with more emphasis on the consonants so that the sound is drawn out slightly longer, like the second, dissonant chord in the sonata. I stare for a minute before responding. "So I know you?" I say stupidly, stuttering over the words. "Yeah, you know me." He is drunk, and tries to walk forward but trips over himself, like Bach's winding run of notes that seems to be heading nowhere in particular. He places his fat white hand on the brown countertop in front of where I am standing and drums his pink fingers on the greasy linoleum. If I didn't know better, the quick movement of his hands would have reminded me of those of a harpsichordist. The taciturn Mexican briefly looks up and exhales slowly before turning back to his paper. The silence is unbearable. "I want some fucking onion rings." I can see the headlights of his car through the front window. He is double-parked. I nod and turn on the fryer, a little frustrated at having to work at this hour. The golden oil hisses and little pricks of heat land on my skin, like popping sixteenth notes.

As the sonata develops, it gains intensity, with impressive technical ornamentations fleshing out the musical theme, presently growing and fluctuating as another person enters. It is a girl wearing faded jeans and too much lipstick. She is much too young to be traveling with the guy at the counter, but she comes up behind him, wraps her arms around his sizable waist, and starts kissing his neck. I cringe and try to concentrate on Bach's mathematical perfection that always draws golden strands of sound from those who attempt to scale the heights of his music. "Get the fuck off me," he tries to say, but it comes out in a slur of words. The whites of her eyes flash at mine and for a minute I can see the fear in them. "But I'm hungry, I want a burrito." She has a whiny voice that is not unlike the high notes of a violin when played sourly, which they often are. He is silent and I feel sorry for her so I take a tortilla from under the counter and open a new bag of iceberg lettuce. I begin making the burrito and am just about to ask "Chicken or beef?" when the Mexican, who has never before uttered a word in my presence, begins to sing in Spanish: a sad, discursive Mexican folk song. The guy at the counter is too drunk now to notice, but the girl eyes the Mexican suspiciously. "Hey," she whines, "hey, what's the idea?" The impatient, confused tone in her voice makes me angry, and I hurriedly spread the prepackaged cheese and salsa onto the tortilla.

Notes expand and build, then die down again, the theme being repeated now in double-stops and unresolved chords. The guy's blue eyes flutter for a second and then grow blank. He moans briefly and then shrugs onto the girl's shoulder. She has a hard time holding him up and finally lets him lie, facedown, on the counter. I decide to make it a vegetarian burrito and open up the canned refried beans, slopping on sour cream and guacamole. The Mexican's song has now floated into a lovely falsetto; he is trying to imitate the woman's part in what is clearly a couple's love duet. His voice cracks and I cannot help but smile.

I finish up the burrito and wrap it in wax paper and hand it to the distraught girl, who is kneeling over her companion. She quietly thanks me; Bach continues his melodious journey onward and upward. My mind floats back to the guy's comment to me. Where did I know him from? How did he know me? The questions swirl in my head like the chunks of vegetables in the salsa. I take another look at his thin pale hair and his folded skin. Something about him touches within me the image I carry in my soul of the Great Composer: each carrying the heavy burden of a difficult life on his stout shoulders, yet each touched with a sort of divine magnetism. Is the same force that draws me toward the music now drawing me toward this mysterious visitor? I feel a strange sympathy for him. The melody of the Mexican's song now seems to have left this world and ascended to heaven, momentarily distracting me from my questions.

The sonata becomes jerky and abrupt. The girl is gulping down her burrito. It looks as if she has forgotten her companion for the moment. I look at her for a moment, trying to watch the pulverized burrito descend down her achy throat into her stomach. A strange curiosity compels me to ask the girl his name. Avoiding eye contact, she responds as if from far away, "Carl Philipp Emanuel."

Everything stops — the song, the wind outside, the smell of his breath. Or maybe my mind has just blocked it all out at the sound of the guy's name. I look up slowly, not believing what I have just heard. "What?" I barely manage to say.

"Carl Philipp Emanuel," she says again, loudly and annoyingly. Suddenly his head jerks up and he is able to weakly ask for water. In a daze I fill up a Styrofoam cup and help her bring him to a table. I sit across from him and watch as he gulps down the cool water. He looks at me with those angry eyes again, and I stare, incredulous, at a man with the exact same name as Bach's son.

"What the hell are you looking at?" he somehow sputters out. I am speechless. He shields his eyes suddenly and grasps his forehead, digging his harpsichordist nails into the flesh. I can hear the Mexican's song again and it has reached a level of almost ecstatic joy. The intensity of the moment is too much for me to bear, and I feel prickles of heat dancing up my spine and over my face. His headache seems to have died down and he can speak again, although he is obviously reluctant. "So what if I am his fucking relative? Where the fuck has it gotten me?" I cannot believe the words coming out of his mouth. The descendent of the source of the most complex and beautiful concepts ever created is sitting in front of me: a drunk, profane molester who has no idea of the divine splendor running through his veins.

"How am I different from this place?" he demands unexpectedly. "Selling people what you call Mexican food." My eyes widen, the Mexican's chest is now swelling in song, pure and exquisite. "Fucking hundreds of years of history while you package burritos in plastic like it was shit." His fat pink finger shoots to the Mexican in the corner. "The same fucking place where that song comes from. We're peas in a fucking pod, man." He grabs his head again. Fortissimo chord. To the girl, "Let's get the hell out of here." The girl looks at him like she is seeing him for the first time. "OK," she whispers. They stagger out of their seats and through the front door. The double-parked car screeches into the windy night. The smell of burning onion rings sizzles from the fryer.

The sonata ends as it begins, with a G-minor chord. It is not angry like the beginning, however; it imparts the restless feeling of unsettling calm. I am silent in my seat, my eyes still open wide and incredulous. After what seems like forever, fermata over the final chord, I turn achingly slowly toward the now silent Mexican. He is reading his paper and, like salsa on a tortilla, a grand smile is spread over his lips.

— Leon Hilton

217

Mothers and Comforters

"She doesn't respect me," he complained. "She's changed a lot from when she was younger."

My father sought comfort in the only sympathetic set of ears in the house. My mother was the problem he complained about, my brother didn't care about anyone's problems but his own, and I was often too tired to tell him that I was quickly learning not to care, either.

"She treats me like I'm inferior, like she's the boss."

They fought regularly. He claimed that he never fought with her but backed down to keep her from getting upset. He claimed to allow my mother her tantrums because he knew she would never let him be right. I pointed out the possibility that his silent capitulation only made things worse. He denied it and continued to use me for his sounding board.

"If it weren't for you and me, Dad probably would have left a while ago," my brother often said.

"Every time I even open my mouth, she starts yelling. I just opened my mouth. That's it. It's like I'm a kid, like I did something wrong."

I drowned him out, nodding every few minutes. He kept talking, relieved to find such a rapt audience.

My attention was elsewhere.

When my mother came to wake me, she had a grim, scary expression on her face. I shrank back into my pillow for a second, certain I'd done something to upset her.

"Grandpa's dead," she said, and then she was gone. I sat up in my bed and mulled over what she'd said.

"Grandpa's dead." What did that mean? Who was my grandpa? My father told me that I'd met him once, when I was four, but I still didn't know who he was.

"Grandpa's dead." What was I supposed to do now? Should I cry? Should I be sad?

I went to my mother's dresser and stared into the mirror. Scrunching up my face, I tried as hard as I could to cry, but all I could think about was what was on TV that morning, and how much my face hurt from trying to cry.

Mom came and found me then, and made me get dressed. I remembered that Grandpa was her daddy, so I watched her to see how I should react. But she was quiet, and her face didn't move, so I was quiet, and I kept my face as still as possible. I failed, and tugged playfully on her pinky to console myself.

Later, we went to Grandpa's apartment in Chinatown. It was very small and everything smelled of Chinese herbs. I didn't like the smell, but I liked poking at the little ivory carvings on his shelf. Daddy said they were Buddhas and Mom said they weren't for me and made me sit on the narrow, smelly bed while she talked to the lawyer. I thought it was strange but acceptable that she didn't let Daddy ask any questions. After all, Grandpa was her dad, not his. She finished talking to the lawyer and told Daddy to get the car started.

When we got home, Mommy bundled up Grandpa's comforter that smelled of Chinese herbs and put it in the washing machine. She said she would use it for my bed.

When I was little, I used to have a recurring nightmare. In that nightmare, I would be walking down the street with my hand tucked into my mother's, and she would disappear.

Sometimes, I would catch glimpses of her in the distance as I ran down the pavement, calling for her. Sometimes, a strange man would appear and give me a black plastic comb. Sometimes, my father would appear and take my hand, and I would pull away and run down the street to look for Mom. Sometimes, my brother would come and make fun of me for making Mom go away, and I would wake up screaming at the air over my bed, Eric sleeping soundly in his own room.

Sometimes, I would get up in the middle of the night and peek through the door that separated my room from my parents' just to make sure she hadn't really left.

I never understood the comb.

I looked up, my hands lost in the folds of the blue comforter.

Mom finished plucking the lint off her side and waited impatiently for me to finish mine. She was sitting in the sun, and it reminded me of how I'd always known I was unique: My mother was Chinese, but her hair was more red than brown and her eyes turned green in the sun.

"Hurry up," she urged me. I redoubled my efforts and she smiled a little, her mood shifting as swiftly as a chameleon's skin. "Remember when you were little, and we took you to Hong Kong? Remember how you used to play with my grandmother? Remember the yellow comforter?"

Yes. I continued working.

"Remember when we visited your father's sister? Number eight?"

I shook my head, no. I'd been too young then. I didn't remember.

"I'm done."

I lifted my hands to my face and held them under my nose. They smelled faintly of herbs.

I became impatient, listening to my father's litany. Turning on him, I snapped out a biting remark, essentially dismissing him as I might a younger child. Hurt, he closed his mouth and looked away.

Later, I wrote an essay about my greatest fear, churning out emotionless strings of drivel about the distance between the top of the Statue of Liberty and the ground far below. But in my nightmare, I called out to my father and he turned stiffly towards me.

And his face took on the same sullen cast he often used to greet my mother.

And I became her.

It was a sign of weakness, for me. Crying was for children and lifeless people. I'd read books that seemed to support that belief — science fiction/fantasy novels, adventure books, children's books about honor and glory, radiating from the hero of some nonsensical war — and I imagined that, since it applied so often to the world of literature, it must therefore apply to life.

My face was red and puffy.

A string of ill luck, an unexpected rejection, and a depression that sank in too quickly to have come from nowhere; I collapsed into a chair in my dining room and my mother cracked a rare joke, teasingly accusing me of lying about some inconsequential thing. I cried. I put my head down on my folded arms and struggled to remain quiet, but muffled tears somehow draw more attention than open sobbing, and soon enough, my mother was tentatively touching my hair.

"It's okay," she murmured. "You see? That's why you shouldn't lie." She kept up the joke because she didn't know what to do. I didn't blame her. I'd made her uncomfortable.

Later I went up to my room and lay facedown on my bed. My brother stopped in my door and asked me if I was all right. Angrily, I told him to go away. Then I pushed my face as far into the soft thickness of my comforter as possible, breathing deeply.

I couldn't smell the Chinese herbs anymore, but almost . . .

She was upset. Somehow, in some way, I had managed to upset my mother. And the worst part was that I didn't even know what I'd done.

My mother didn't get upset very often, but when she did, it was like running through a minefield with bare feet and a one-ton weight precariously balanced on each shoulder.

"I'm leaving," she snapped. "I'm going away."

Mom certainly did go through the motions. She stalked over to the closet and retrieved her jacket, then snagged her purse and turned into the door of our apartment.

"Mommy, wait! Mommy!"

I tried tears, but they never worked on her. My brother was no help, either, just an awful, sullen silence at my back.

"Bye, I'm going."

The lock clicked once and the door opened, letting in a whoosh of Chinese takeout and pizza from the floor below us, and it was as if every nightmare I'd ever had came roaring through that door on the stale air.

"Mommy!"

I gave up, finally, and dropped to the floor, wrapping my arms around her leg. I felt like the shipwrecked sailor who clutched in vain at the broken mast of his ship as the waves pulled it slowly from his grasp.

"You have to learn to respect me. You have to learn to be good. Otherwise, I'll leave and that's it — no more Mommy."

She locked the door again and stepped back inside. I let go of her leg as she dropped her bag and jacket. She hadn't left. But it didn't really matter to me. I kept crying, and she continued to scold me through my tears. She almost had. It didn't matter that she didn't leave, because she almost did.

"You people don't do anything! I get home and I'm tired and I don't even get to sit down first! Work, work, work! You people don't appreciate me!"

The shouting went on for a while, though she addressed an empty room. Daddy had gone to the basement, and Eric and I had both retreated to our rooms.

I could still hear her through my closed door.

"Edwina!"

"Coming!" I flung open the door and raced down the stairs

as quietly as I could without sacrificing speed, in order to appease her in some small way.

I didn't dare drown out her muttering.

If I were younger, I would have cried. Instead, I fled back up to my room after dinner and stared at my hands for a while. After an hour of sitting in the dark, I imagined I felt something sharp cut lengthwise down my wrists. I cursed and stuffed my hands under my pillow until the stinging went away.

I look up at her, arms wrapped around her leg. No tears this time. She petted my hair and I rested my head on her knee, fingers curled possessively around the shrunken calf of her right leg, a remnant of her childhood bout with polio.

"You were a much prettier baby than your brother," she said. "He was born bald. You had hair."

I giggled, laughing both at her and with her. That was allowed, sometimes, provided you stepped cautiously, carefully watching the ground on which you trod.

"You were a much better baby than Eric," she said. "He kicked me in the face. You always smiled for the pictures."

I laughed again, content in that moment when laughter was allowed. My brother shouted at us from the living room, then joined my father in screaming at the Knicks. I looked up and said something stupid, like: "Men. They're such babies."

She just laughed.

I once read a story about a lonely warrior who managed to save everyone but herself. Late at night, I imagined myself to be her, determined to rewrite her story.

In my dream, my mother's face hovered over mine, and I woke before the warrior could save herself.

Damned again.

I remember how once, when I was little, I was in the kitchen, bugging Mom while she prepared dinner. A commercial came on TV about an upcoming special on ancient Egypt. I jumped in front of Mom and started doing the Egyptian, one hand in front, one hand in back, elbows and wrists at right angles.

She laughed then, too.

"Mom's mental," said Eric, tugging on my ponytail.

"Who cares?"

I hugged Dad, startling him out of his doze as the Yankees came up for bat in the bottom of the sixth. He jerked upright, patting my arm and glancing nervously at the closed door, beyond which my mother, who thought baseball was "stupid," was watching her soaps.

"Who cares?" I asked again. "I don't."

Privately, I wondered. The blue comforter was still on my bed, and I was still the only one who could make her laugh.

I wondered if the laughter was still hollow.

— Edwina Lui

Sundays

"Cross your legs,"
my mother whispers,
but I figure I've got nothing
to hide.
So I sit on the pew
with knees spread wide
and tiny scuffed shoes
dangling high
above marble floors.

I gaze past the altar
to the mosaic Mary,
always on the verge of tears.
She floats weightless
alongside angels
with bellies bigger than mine.
So why do her eyes seem so sad?
She's in the sky,
but I'm trapped down here,
staring at the votive candles,
letting my eyes glaze over
'til each light is haloed
and colors blur.

A draft whirls above my head,
carrying with it
the drone of the organ
and the priest's monotone.
I stare at him and pretend
I'm absorbing
his sermon deep in my soul,
but really I'm just wondering
what he's got
beneath his long white robe.
Does his mother make him
wear his Sunday best?
Or does he stand comfortably
in last night's pajamas,
laughing inside at all of us
who rose hours earlier
to be shampooed
and scrubbed clean
of all our weekend sins,
then stuffed into starched suits
to cover the dirt
that won't wash off in the tub.

— Jennifer Strunge

Montserrat

for my grandfather Joseph

I.

This island reminded you of home,
emerald hills swelled like the stomachs of pregnant women,
the acacias and evergreens caught on a wind's note,
holding fruit between their limbs. Sunlight cut
through the sky like colorful diamonds. The horizon floated
along the ocean's mouth, boats bobbed into the sunset like children's play
    toys.

Your oldest brother, Francis, learned to hear the sea.
He spent days on the boat, smelling sun, burned flesh,
lemon juice. He learned the names of the tropical fish —
red snapper, cod, gar, angel and king — how to maneuver his way
through mid-afternoon tide and the host of tourists and fishermen
who swarmed like flies.

There was always something to scale, gut and sell.
His hands became stiff from the hauling of ropes,
the sinking of nets and hooks into his flesh. His muscles gave out.
A hurricane brought a rudder flying into the back of his head.

Your youngest brother, Colin, was taken by the Arawaks
and the mass of darker skin: beige, gold, bronze, mocha, ebony.
He took books and recipes to read the folklore and spells

of the *obeah* man: how to appease the *jumbi,* the spirits of ancestry,
how to soothe burns with coconut oil, spider bites with pulp of aloe plant,
two dosages of cod liver oil night and day to rid parasites and viruses,
molasses for sore throat and heartburn
and ginger root tea for long lives.

II.

You decided to own land. You paid your debts.
With brothers' help, you invested in liquor.
You were sober enough,
to set down your pipe and novels
to juggle papayas and guavas,
holding them like the breasts of a woman you needed.

In the marketplace you searched out your wife.
A straw basket was perched on her head, full of gifts.
One brown arm kept it in place, the other held her balance.
You loved the way her arm filled out the curve of her hip,
how she moved like water.

Two nights later, you brought her to the beach
and climbed the cliffs together
to watch the clouds gather in the dark distance
and pulsate over the ocean.
You laid her beside you, dusted sand from her legs and stomach,
and counted each star for each piece of clothing. . . .

III.

You were all early ghosts — Francis, Joseph and Colin.
Your blood was claimed long before your mother
gave birth to you in Ballyshannon, long before
your uncle, the Catholic priest, christened you near Donegal Bay.

You promised your children a different life.
You set Yeats and Joyce at their sides,
telling them to press the words to their brains and ears,
to memorize, to hear the music
drifting from the piano,
creaking through the mahogany stairwell,
and white-washed walls.

They watched the liquid shoot up
like flying fish into your lungs, your hands
propped like pillows on your belly, telling you to
breathe Papa, feeding you with spoons,
reading to you until their eyes gave way to sleep.
You never thanked them.

One by one they left saying, *daddy, I will forget you.*
They blinked away time
like the switching of TV channels.
And when you watched the birds glide under the sky,
the sun sinking like a pot of gold, smelled the bay rum,
yellow poui and pink coral, listened to the ocean hurl
itself against the cliffs in a drunken rage, you thought of death —
Paul, split open again and again by his boat and the breakers,

Colin's young heart collapsing, the herbs and cures
that couldn't stop the drink.

Now all the seams of your life have worn away
and sent your sons and daughters far away from here.

— Jamilah Ryan

Alex

Alex sat behind me in math. Sometimes I'd lend him one of my pencils, and when I got it back, the eraser would be worn down to a nub, his nervous teeth marks scattering the wood with shallow dents. His fingernails were always grubby. It was surprising to hear his voice, as he rarely spoke, and when he did it was always in short, unpunctuated sentences. He smelled like oranges.

It must have been about a month or so after my brother got sick that Alex started giving me parts of his lunch. I never saw him in the cafeteria; I don't know where he went for that twenty-minute slice of time every day. But at the end of math he'd shove a rumpled paper bag across my desk before scrambling out the door like he had somewhere important to go. Inside the bag would be the dessert his mother had packed him that morning: a Twinkie, a cupcake, sometimes a baggie full of gumdrops or jelly beans. I'd walk home, my cheeks filled with sugar or frosting, crumpling the paper bag with his name written across it in slanted printing, throwing it at the big sycamore in the schoolyard as hard as I could. Walking and eating slowly, to make both last.

The night before Eddie's funeral it snowed. I fled from the house, shuffling between the sickly yellow circles the streetlights made on the ground. The plows were just starting to rumble down the street, pushing the snow aside like dinosaurs. There was a terrible dark song in my head that I couldn't remember any of the words to. It leaned hard on my brain, and I wondered what would happen if I just exploded right there in front of Mrs. Robinson's white-capped lawn gnomes, my whole body going up like fireworks for some unannounced holiday, the sparks sizzling against the snow as they fell. I thought about all the violent things I could do with so much snow: bombard cars with white missiles, destroy snowmen, bury the town with a huge white wave.

That was when I felt the snowball smack against my neck and slither down the back of my coat. I whirled around, expecting someone amazing: God or the devil standing there in a snowsuit and mittens, grinning sardonically at the trick he had played on me. What would he do once I saw him? Would he lift me up and carry me away from all this dark, or would he meet my nose with a right hook, delivering me swiftly into the arms of the snowbank?

Alex stood there, shifting in his oversized rubber boots. It was too dark for me to read his face, but I could see well enough to hit my target. He didn't look surprised when I slammed him with a fistful of snow. He stepped back a little to keep his balance but lost it instead, sliding across the white ground until he landed in a sprawl across the sidewalk. His laughter broke over me like a thousand tiny bells, but instead of crystal they were made of spun sugar that shattered into a sparkling deluge.

When our fingernails were raw from scraping snow and our throats were hoarse from laughing, we started walking. The yellow lights of the plows flickered through the blackness like steady fireflies. We stomped through the snow in silence, our breath billowing in puffs ahead of us as if we were dragons or steam engines. Standing at my front door, watching Alex's back slowly blur into the blackness, I could see our side-by-side sets of footprints, clear and deep on the sidewalk, going on forever in the snow.

That was all.

Later that year, his dad got a job in Sacramento. I passed by the moving truck on my bike as it rumbled out of town. The driver wore a Phillies cap and a splash of stubble on his chin. I didn't see Alex. The truck whushed by, blowing up the first few dead leaves of autumn in its wake. They fluttered against the wheels of my bike like brittle butterflies before settling on the road.

In school in the fall, there were new kids who filled up all the empty seats in the classrooms. Autumn was longer than usual, and its warmth cut into winter, making for a soggy New Year's, with sidewalks still cluttered with dead leaves that shuffled into the gutters and clogged the street grates. Winter's driving rains turned to spring's mild deluges, and the crocuses crept out of the ground as if to say that nothing had ever changed. But that year in math, I crossed out all my mistakes instead of erasing them, and my pencils were still dotted with teeth marks.

— Kendra Levin

Guffy

I can see my own eyes as they were when I was little. They were the rich color of Hershey's dark chocolate and they had no center. All my grins were toothless and my hair was so curly it was free or in the process of escaping.

My older brother was Superman on Sunday, Batman on Monday, Spiderman on Tuesday, and then the cycle continued. He was Clark Kent with or without the costume; his Coke-bottle glasses and Mickey Mouse ears discouraged anyone from thinking he was anything more than a mere boy. I was smarter than most people; I knew of his powers.

When we were bubbles we took baths; when we were soldiers we watched G.I. Joe. His glasses got thicker and his ears got bigger and I thought his head might outweigh his body and break him in half. Ironically, it wasn't his ears or his glasses that enervated him. It was his lungs. Dust, smoke, or the act of trying to catch me as I broke into a run would start his coughing. Coughing would lead to gasping, gasping to a sound I had never heard before. It was a sucking sound, the sound of an animal stuck in a plastic bag. My brother lived in a world where air didn't exist; he was a fish out of water.

Many days out of our months and many nights out of our days were spent either in hospitals or rushing to hospitals. At night before I would fall asleep I would listen for any whimpering coming from his room because I knew that's how it started. Unlike the recessiveness of his asthmatic breathing, his crying would increase with his pain. Whimpering led to crying, crying to sobbing, and lastly, sobbing to choked screaming, like a cat being hung on a clothesline. He didn't understand not being able to breathe. His superheroes could inhale and exhale like pros; why couldn't he? His breathing was a never-ending battle that didn't involve capes or batarangs or scaling walls. It involved his lungs.

One night I woke up to screaming. It wasn't the scream of a murder; it wasn't high-pitched and keen and straight like an arrow. It was lower and longer, wavering in and out and over invisible hills, a lost banshee looking for its life, looking for me. I got up to go to his room but by then my dad was carrying him downstairs. My mom pushed me back to my room, back to sleep, and I heard the guttural engine sound of my father's VW van starting up.

The walls were white and cold. The floor shone up at me, reflecting the fluorescent lights above and revealing nothing. We walked and walked and the heels of my mother's shoes echoed and were lost in telephones and people's voices. We reached the room and my father walked in, followed by my mother and me. I didn't look at the bed or who was in it; I kept my eyes to the floor and walked over to a steel radiator under the window. I distinctly remember the feel of the metal grates as I lifted myself on top of it. It was chilly, like bare skin touching snow, and the lines left an imprint on the backs of my thighs and my memory.

"Flossie?" I raised my head. He was lying in the bed, covers pulled up to his chin, eyes partially opened. An oxygen mask was on his face and many tubes ran in and out of his wrists. I wanted to cry but I didn't. I didn't cry for Superman when he was exposed to kryptonite; you don't cry for fallen heroes simply because you know they'll win. Lex Luthor always ended up pounding rocks in prison; the Joker finished his reign of terror on Gotham City splattered on the sidewalk. But in the same vein, without villains, how would superheroes exist? That was why Lex Luthor always made bail and Catwoman replaced the Joker. That was why my brother's lungs would always be weak. It was that simple, and at the age of five or six I was made to know it. I hated knowing it. I fully believe that was the day my eyes developed their center and my curly hair straightened enough to make the passive black waves I now possess.

"Hi, Guffy." I smiled and he smiled back through his mask. I could never pronounce Geoff or Geoffrey and I was the only one allowed to call him that.

"Come over here." He patted the bed and I slid off the radiator and climbed up next to him. "You shouldn't be so sad. It's actually kind of cool here. They've got video games down the hall and if I wanna play the nurse can just wheel me in." He pointed to a small wheelchair in the corner. I looked at him and smiled weakly; my bedridden hero not able to fly.

My brother came home after a couple of days, but suddenly it was all in slow motion. Our playing lost its innocence because I was too busy watching him. I watched him inhale and exhale; I watched him laugh and cry and breathe and breathe. I watched him from the newly developed center of my eyes; he *became* the center of my eyes. Gradually his attacks lessened, pretty soon they didn't exist, and in no time whatsoever he was running and jogging like a normal, healthy boy. His lungs have grown stronger and the gasping has stopped. But still, I watch him. His glasses are gone and although he will never fully grow into his enormous ears, he at least looks normal. But when I see him, when I *really* see him, I see the little boy with features too dramatic for his face. I see the older brother who was a G.I. Joe, who was a seeker when I was the hider, who had a cape for every superhero that could fly. I see the grinning face of a bug-eyed little boy, waiting up for Santa and sitting next to a girl with her wild hair and bottomless eyes.

— Florence Arend

Chutney

C

Is for crazy, cracking, and crippled. C is for Mr. Caziz. Also for his face that has wrinkles like ravines that spread spidery over his face. They flood with water when he sweats and gush down a salty rapid until it drops gray off his chin. Crippled because his left arm goes only to the elbow and then stops in a red ball. A jagged bone sticks out and cries, "I want to get out, I want to be a hand!" But it always stays one knobby stump poking out of a white-collared shirt. "Crazy!" yells Mr. Caziz at anyone, so that they look back and know that the man with an ornament for a hand and a cracked face is capital C for crazy.

The one hand of Mr. Caziz is somehow connected to a brain that can shoot out calculations. And luckily for him, his wife was endowed with two able hands that can shoot out a chutney that will play jingle bells on your tuna and dribble a sweet nectar down your throat. Together they opened a store. A store with was-white walls splotched with colors that spin together like amoebas dancing. Where cha-chink cha-chink tings the air when slap slap green bills pass from one porcelain customer hand to one big brown hand with square fingernails and callused knuckles or one slender pistachio hand with butter cream palms.

H

Is for hypothetical, honey, and horseradish. Hypothetical situations normally stay hypothetical. But I needed money to keep my empty stomach from avenging me in the night or turning into a purple prune that would float up and choke me. Hypothetical became reality. A job to keep me alive and whatnot for the crying raging floating person I call Mother. The one with skin like gooey honey and a mouth that in dreams sprouts arms which strangle me. A job at the chutney shop with Caziz. Over apple juice I decided that for my mother and myself I must go sell fruity mixtures for people to spoon and dollop onto delectable meats. My mother said, "That is horseradish! You don't have to go!" But then again my mother said that in India cows fly and my father was FDR.

This morning the air is a wet blanket. Warm and dead it collapses on my shoulders. Sticky sticky the clouds are cotton candy starting to drip melt into pools of pink sugar. Slurp, my shirt licks at my skin as I peel it away. Mr. Caziz wears a white shirt with a stiff collar. It sags into pouty lips over his banana pakoora belly. Clear circles spill out from under his arms and tiny beads like oil sit on his fat upper lip. Choppy words tell me do this, don't do that. I didn't realize there were so many types of chutney.

U

Is for ugly, umbrella, and understand. Mr. Caziz tells his wife her ankles are showing. A plum-purple sari with a tiny yellow hem swish swishes at her tiny feet. "Ugly! Ugly!" he yells at her. Sour breath steams between his two front teeth that have a gap through which I could spit. He is an ugly clown with even uglier words. Mrs. Caziz tucks her arms under her sari and snaps shut. Click! like a purple umbrella. When the ugly one is away Mrs. Caziz tells me how to make chutney. She shows me her fruit and hands me a mango. I bite and its juice spurts onto my cheeks, lips, and hands. Golden juice skis down my chin and jumps onto my collarbones. Mrs. Caziz laughs because she understands and is happy because I am.

Every day I come in and sit on the papaya-green stool. My thighs glue to it and smack their lips as I shift my weight. A woman comes in with a voice that sparkles like champagne. Her eyes are blue like every ocean colliding with an April sky. Mrs. Caziz takes one look at her and disappears down the stairs. The woman sings her order to me, and the coins sing back as they tinkle into her hands. When she is gone, Mrs. Caziz comes back upstairs.

T

Is for terrifying, tenacious, and tiki. Mr. Caziz, renamed Ugly Monster, stomps up the stairs. He rubs his stump of an arm and yells for Mrs. Caziz.

"That sthhtupid ungrateful woman . . . that sthcandalous . . ." His tongue flops around, shooting spit at me like a rapid-fire machine gun. Mrs. Caziz silently appears from the back room. He grabs her and his face is terrifying. Shining forehead and sausage lips sneer as he drags her one-handed into the store-room. Boom! Tock tock tock, boom! The clock on the wall beats out the time into the stillness. I pick up a feather duster and swipe at the shelves. I rearrange the chutneys and fix the sign on the door. I open the register, Ca-ching. Boom! Tock tock tock, boom! Time drags on. Mr. Caziz is tenacious, but he is longer with her now than ever before. I pick at my shirt. Cart-wheeling tiki flowers leapfrog over my stomach and shimmy onto my chest.

N

Is for nowhere, nothing, and nobody. Finally, Mr. Caziz pulls open the door and I frantically try to look busy. He barely glances my way before stomping down the stairs. I want to spring to the back room and see that sagging plum, which I'm afraid the ugly monster has crushed. But I wait. Pickled can-taloupe, sugar, salt, vinegar, water . . . the ingredients of a jar blur when I hear a door slowly creak open. It is Mrs. Caziz. One purple flower has bloomed on her eye, deep to match her sari. A bowl of alphabet soup catches in my throat when I see her. She shuffles over with her head lowered and starts to un-load a crate of jars.

"Mrs. Caziz . . ." I slosh out her name.

"Find the new batch of pineapple for me, dear," she whispers.

I hesitate and then search through a box labeled JULY 4TH. I find the jar and it sits cool in my hand. Reaching over I put it on the shelf above her head. When my arm comes near, her head ducks in like a turtle. I know Mrs. Caziz came to America with her husband. She has no other family. She is nowhere, has nothing and nobody.

E

Is for empty, egg, and elephant. Mrs. Caziz walks around like a wicker cane. Black satellite dishes grow under her eyes. She is empty like a dry well, and my words bounce off her bottom like dead pebbles. I can make twenty kinds of chutney now. Mrs. Caziz hands me a mango to peel and slice. The only time she doesn't purse her lips so they turn white at the tips is when we are cooking. I say nothing, afraid to crack her. She is an egg and I'm afraid to spill out her yolk.

Crash!

"Damn it! Who put that flowerpot there?" yells Mr. Caziz. Mrs. Caziz's lips curl ever so slightly. I flick the black seeds into a yellow bowl and try to keep from laughing. Mr. Ugly Monster tramps up the stairs and snorts through his nose. His skin is tough and peeling. His big feet clunk over to me where I cower because he is the elephant and I am the mouse.

Y

Is for young, yellow, and yo-yo. Mrs. Caziz tells me she wishes she was my age. She tells me to stay young and put my time in a bubble where I can reach it anytime. Her bubble smells like saffron. Her wrists shake and her bangles clink against each other as her face relaxes. Little monkey hands branch out from the corner of her eyes when she smiles.

Carelessly peeling fruit, Mrs. Caziz tells me about her old home. "My favorite vendor sold nuts under the bedroom window. Oh! And the magazine man on the corner who had greasy hair and skin like melting cheese poori . . ."

The sun plays hopscotch across the sky, and I glance at the clock. I don't want to stop her trail of words and make her tired and yellow again. Nervously, I cross and uncross my ankles. My fingers itch at mosquito bites, making them swollen and bloated like red fish gone belly-up.

"Close up!" a voice booms from down below. Mrs. Caziz opens her mouth in surprise and then hops off her chair.

She fingers her sari and apologizes, "I'm sorry, I don't know where the time went."

I want to plead with her not to be sorry, that I loved seeing her happy. When she hesitantly looks up, I beg into her almond eyes. Like a tiny flutter, her head bobs up and nods to me. It's like a cashew yo-yo on a macadamia string. Dinner and the heat are preoccupying me. Some little bee has flown inside my head and will not stop buzzing. I look at Mrs. Caziz as I pull open the door to leave. As she stoops over the shelves, I notice how much she is starting to resemble the chutney that she makes.

— Carrie Vasios

Three Ways of Remembering

I. Concerto in E Minor

Fugue

Salvage your sundress from a wire hanger in the back of your closet. Note how its blue flowers bring out the blue in your eyes. Fred has never said anything about your eyes. Maybe tonight will be the night. More than anything you want to hear him say, "Sarah, you have the most gorgeous eyes." Paste your lips in pastel pink, and tongue the lipstick from your front tooth. Now smile. Thirty more minutes until you meet Fred. Decide to waste time on a cup of coffee. Copy Fred's new cell phone number onto the side of your hand; you may need to get in touch with him. Slap on your sandals and catch a taxi. Inside it smells like the city: smoke and sweat laced with week-old lunch meat. Tell the driver to stop at the coffee shop beside the bus station. The brakes scream as he lunges to a stop. Give him a twenty-dollar tip.

You sit at the table closest to the window so you can watch the people. A woman stands with her back facing you. The wind parts her hair, and it dances like smoke signals around her face. It's the color of a rich cherry wood, polished to reflect light like a mirror. Your hair is straight and brown. You finger the ends and notice where they've split. Two tables down, a man and a woman argue about the tip.

Forget the coffee. It probably wouldn't have been good anyway. You want the bus. All you can think about is your head against the back of the ugly velour seats. A voice over the inter-com rasps the next arrivals and departures. Listen carefully. Approach the clerk behind the window and ask for a one-way ticket to San Francisco. Explain how you've always wanted to see the Golden Gate. Forget that you're thirty and still hold your breath when you cross over a bridge. The clerk pushes his brows together and wrinkles a smile. Tell him your credit card is bad. Ask for scissors. Write a check for the ticket, and leave your license with the balding man. Throw away your check-book. Give your watch to the man with the open guitar case. It's been thirty minutes.

Invention

Buy a box of red hair color from the drugstore next door. It's the permanent kind, not the type that will brass and then wash away in twenty-four days. You want the red to breed in your hair. You want to saturate yourself in crimson. Lock yourself in the bathroom and wash your hair in the sink; now paste the color onto your hair, slathering each strand with the pink foam. Wait twenty minutes, and then rinse it out. Your hair can air dry. Outside the bathroom, two women are pacing. Neither seems content, and you race away as they dive for the door, squawking at each other.

Find your seat on the bus, even though it doesn't leave for another thirty minutes. Trace your fingers across the stripes on the back of the seat in front of you; note how the velour changes color as you stroke it back and forth against your hand. Outside, the day is cooling as clouds shade the sun. Finger the lace at the bottom of your dress. It is ripping on the left side; you do nothing but make the rip longer. Circle the tear around your hem until the lace falls to your ankles. Throw it out the window.

A man sits next to you. The seat sighs as air speeds from the cushion. Introduce yourself as Albany Drake. Let the L roll off your tongue in a wave, and snap the K. Nod inwardly, satisfied with the way it sounds. His right eyebrow arches upward as he seems to taste your name. He introduces himself as Rosco Phillips. Rosco has dark hair that rises in a small, gelled arch, then smoothes down above his ears. You repeat the name to yourself, as if to convince him that maybe you won't remember it. Settle into coyness; cross your legs, and situate yourself in a diagonal across the seat. Dance your foot in the air as you ask him if he's married. He's not. When he asks if you are seeing anyone, tell him no, and honestly believe it.

The bus pulls from the station as you tell Rosco of your childhood in San Francisco, of how you used to run across the Golden Gate Bridge once a week just to see the sun rise. He seems impressed and invites you to give him a tour of the city. You oblige but warn him that it's been twenty years since you've been to California, and there are places you most likely won't remember. He says he doesn't mind and offers to buy you dinner the next day. Tell him that sounds nice, then turn away and chase the buildings outside with your eyes as the bus begins to speed past them. Try to sleep.

When you wake, night has caved into the bus, and Rosco is asleep. He makes a slight groaning noise as he exhales, and you wonder what he's dreaming about. By now, your hair is dry and

247

cold from the bus's air-conditioning. In the wisps of light that run through the bus whenever it passes another car or billboard, you can see its fired mahogany blazing from shadows.

The bus stops, and you pull your purse out from under your chair. You squeeze past Rosco, who is curled into a crescent and breathing heavily. You step off the bus into a station that consists only of a bench and a plastic shelter. There is no sign that tells you where you are, and no people around to ask. This is definitely not San Francisco, but you don't mind. You stretch across the bench and close your eyes in wait for morning.

Restoration

The sun squints blinding spears down to you, throwing you into day. When you moan and stretch the grogginess from your muscles a man standing beside you laughs. You look around and realize you don't know where you are. The man says you're in Lowell, Tennessee. You don't know anyone in Lowell. Look around, see a pay phone in the corner of the shelter; call the number on your hand.

A man answers the phone in a flat voice. Tell him you don't know who he is, but his number is on your hand and you were wondering if he could help you. He says his name is Fred. The phone is fuzzy and the speech comes across broken. You have to repeat yourself three times before he understands. He asks if he's talking to Sarah. The name startles you, and he asks you again. You look down at your sandals — see the scratches on each of the heels from clicking them together. Pull at the hem of your dress and notice where threads are hanging loose to your knees. Once again he asks you if he's talking to Sarah. Twist your hair around your finger and realize that you don't know.

II. Dreaming of Blue

Every time the door opens, blending the outside's warm, blush air to the stagnant cold of the restaurant, Fred jerks his head up expectantly. He has been waiting forty-five minutes for his date, Sarah, to meet him. Already he has eaten through two baskets of bread sticks and gulped three glasses of tea. Twenty minutes ago, he called her house, only to speak with the ring that rolled onward like an open-ended question — a question that, to him, would be answered only in terms of rejection. He returned to his seat and moped into a crouched position, forehead collapsing the origami napkin into a confusion of folds. When he decides to leave, an hour has passed. He slaps some money onto the table and shuffles through the door, into the day. The now heavy pallor of wind warns him of rain as he moves homeward.

Once home, Fred falls into a stupor that lasts through the night. He curls under his blankets and pulls all thoughts of Sarah to the front of his mind. He wants to bathe in his rejection. In his pocket is a case that held a necklace. He had intended to give it to Sarah in remembrance of their one-year anniversary. The necklace was small but beautiful. It hung in silver radiance with a tiny tear-shaped cobalt that dropped from the chain. Blue was Sarah's favorite color. He loved seeing her in blue because it brought out the color in her eyes. Sarah had the most gorgeous eyes he had ever seen. A few days ago he realized he had never told her that. In a way, he was scared. If he came on too strong, even after a year, she might leave him. Even so much as praising her eyes could get to be overwhelming, because he knew he wouldn't just stop with her eyes. He knew he would flatter and praise her from her eyes and her hair on down to the way her toes grabbed at the ground whenever she walked barefoot. Sure enough, a year had gone by, and finally she decided she didn't like him. Now she was gone.

Fred pulled her picture from out of his nightstand and stared at her, trying to read into her eyes. He maintained this for an hour, studying her picture, letting her expression in the frame answer his questions. He ran scenes of their life together through his mind — remembered their first date, their picnics, the way she always looked at his mouth when he spoke. After a while, he began remembering things that never even happened, like the time they rented a small cottage for a week. They didn't leave the property the entire duration of their stay. They lived off fresh bread and the fruit that grew wild around the little house. By the end of the night, he had convinced himself of this. By the end of the night, they were married with a child who had died at birth.

Fred had just fallen asleep when the phone rang. He answered it only to hear the crackling of long distance. Three times the caller had to repeat herself before he could understand her. Through his delusion, Fred assumed the caller was Sarah. He thought of her calling from the pay phone ten miles down from their cottage. It must have been her surprise for him. Happy anniversary to me, he thought, and saddled the phone onto the receiver. Fred grabbed the necklace box and ran out the door, waving feverishly for a taxi. For a few moments he stood along the side of the street, feet almost stretching into the gutter that ran along the front side of his apartment. When no taxis came, he began running. He ran six miles until he fell from exhaustion. He lay alongside the road for the rest of the day, asleep or passed out, his breath causing the warm air to shiver. A few times people walked past but said nothing, just carefully stepped over him. One man thought to be kind and pushed Fred off the sidewalk to keep him from being injured by a passerby. That afternoon, the air weighed heavily as Fred slept, clutching the necklace box and dreaming of blue.

III. Nocturne in Gray

Somehow, I'm in a holding cell with some kid who says his name is Thomas. He keeps asking me too many questions I don't know. The policeman on guard's mouth is like a gun barrel: He keeps screaming for us to shut up. Thomas is apparently fairly young; he is scared his parents will send him off to boarding school.

The second hand on the clock sounds like a rifle blasting the moments into extinction. Everything about this place revolves around guns. There's a pistol on everyone's hip, a rack of slender bodies in a glass cabinet in the corner. The room I'm in even reminds me of a gun: blistered cold and refined by harshness.

The policeman steps forward, asks me my name. I tell him I can't recall. He asks me four more times, but I'm only able to give him the same response. His fists fire at the table, and he demands I quit acting smart.

Eventually he will realize that I don't know. My mind is an erased blackboard, clouded with milky-white residue. Can I help it that I can't I don't understand this collaborative puzzlement, this blanket of ignorance with which I never asked to be covered?

The clock kills another second and my chair's rails dig levees parallel to my spine. I wonder how much longer this will last.

— Ellen Knight

Where to Find Infinity

I see forever riding everywhere:

In the funnel of rhododendron after
rain, curled and spitting water towards
the tongues of roots that arch out of the earth
like the gray necks of humpbacks rising to inhale —
it drips itself a drink, finds that only the licking
of the descending drops on its leaves keeps it alive;

In the gray wisps of revelation that find themselves
floating between the lines of a poem,
ghosts that haunt after the last line is read,
  and in the scattering to the periods and the crosses on the "t's"
when you try to look directly at the phantoms
to see what they say — like stars that have died
then revived into newborns;

  and in the mirror, crusty-sighted and narrow-eyed,
pillow-headed after I've just woken up.

— Zack Lindsay

A (Love) Poem

Before I begin this poem
I would like to tell you
that I don't mean any of it.
I'm just writing this poem about you,
and not about your hands
and their soft heavy weight
or about the sound of your breathing
in the hours before dawn.
I wouldn't write a poem
about the words you let go
into the well of my ear
like a thin silver thread.
I wouldn't tell anyone
that you don't really know
all the answers
I wouldn't tell anyone
(especially in a poem)
that you taste like silver
and your eyes tell secrets
when they're bleary with sleep.
And I wouldn't tell a soul
how hard my heart beats now
when our eyes meet
by accident.
So maybe I won't
write a poem at all

because all I could say about you
if I don't say that, is:
maybe I love you.

— Celeste LeCompte

I Knew a Boy

When I think of him I think of the scent of raspberries. And the moon. I think of the tide and trees in the dark. Jumping fence-post hurdles in the inky black of an almost winter night. I think of him driving in that comfortable silence as I watched cars go by on the expressway. And how he sensed my sadness and told me to smile. I think of him tying my shoelaces in knots and timing me as I tried, exasperated, to get them undone (four minutes). Him, tucked into the corner of my study, wrapped in a Mexican-print blanket, humming so that the walls vibrated. I think of Adia. I think of how shocked I was that the decor in our rooms matched, down to the flannel sheets. Birthday cards, meticulously chosen, and phone calls for no other reason than to say hello. I see him at my piano. I hear him singing. I smell him. I feel him breathing, the steady, slow rise and fall of his chest under my head. All the syllables. Dirty socks, thrown out my car window at one in the morning after a "study session." I think of bowling. His impish grin and mischievous pranks. An "A." Standing by himself, dressed in lacrosse gear, on the sidelines. There were movies and hugs and advice, cartoon characters and children. I think of him barefoot in the snow, hopping from foot to foot, threatening to wake up the neighborhood. Tousled hair, seeing whose could stand up straighter longer (mine). I think of late-night conversations, falling asleep on the phone as the sun rose. His music. His keys (or glasses or hat or shoes) taken off and put down somewhere where they were inevitably forgotten until it was time to go. Word games. Card games. I think of him in the backseat while I drove, asking me to tell him a secret. Throwing my gloves into the way back of my station wagon. Broken Volvo glove compartments. I think of him decoding dreams. Sandwiches and pizza, ice cream, Scrabble, and those little dice with letters on every side. Breaking things. I think of him dancing, laughing, making me laugh. Standing outside, dressed up, freezing, and eating Pez. He threw bits of candy during class. Inertia, zero seconds, and the annoying way he always got out of everything. I think of the comfort in being myself around him, his quirky, accepting disposition. Adjectives like aristocratic, snooty, and pretentious. Inside jokes. I think of him falling asleep or curling up under blankets. Whispering. I think of the last time he left my house, knowing he wouldn't come back. Not allowing myself to watch him through the window as he strode down the walk. His shirts were always untucked.

— Leah Christie

✳✳✳✳✳✳✳✳✳✳✳✳✳✳✳✳✳✳✳✳✳✳✳✳✳

BE A PUSH AUTHOR. WRITE NOW.

 *is looking for
new authors with stories to tell*

Enter the PUSH Novel Contest for a chance to
get your novel published. You don't have to
have written the whole thing — just sample
chapters and an outline. For full details, check
out the contest area on ***www.thisispush.com***

✳✳✳✳✳✳✳✳✳✳✳✳✳✳✳✳✳✳✳✳✳✳✳✳✳